Record Palace

Record Palace

Susan Wheeler

A NOVEL

Graywolf Press

SAINT PAUL, MINNESOTA

Publication of this volume is made possible in part by a grant provided by the Minnesota State Arts Board, through an appropriation by the Minnesota State Legislature; a grant from the Wells Fargo Foundation Minnesota; and a grant from the National Endowment for the Arts, which believes that a great nation deserves great art. Significant support has also been provided by the Bush Foundation; Target and Mervyn's with support from the Target Foundation; the McKnight Foundation; and other generous contributions from foundations, corporations, and individuals. To these organizations and individuals we offer our heartfelt thanks.

Published by Graywolf Press
2402 University Avenue, Suite 203
Saint Paul, Minnesota 55114
All rights reserved.

www.graywolfpress.org

Published in the United States of America
Printed in Canada

ISBN 1-55597-420-1

2 4 6 8 9 7 5 3 1
First Graywolf Printing, 2005

Library of Congress Control Number: 2004116112

Cover design: Kyle G. Hunter
Cover photographs: LuckyPix/Veer (skyline) and © Corbis. All rights reserved (record album)

To Jack and Annabel:

May your worlds be large with love.

It makes all the difference in the world, at least in the storybooks, whether the hero confronts the dragon or joins him. It makes all the difference in the world what is chosen as the basis of the happily-ever-after. Is it the self-making, self-affirming challenges of the quest, or is it the creature comforts of consumerism and conformity?

JAMES ALAN MCPHERSON

Finally, here is something that is true.
In nineteen hundred sixty-seven
Mayor Daley the First said to Gwendolyn Brooks,
"People think that Picasso hates Chicago,
and that is why he inflicts his pictures on us.
Write a poem for us about Picasso."

CAROLYN KNOX

Chicago sizzled in the late summer. Just after Labor Day, the gray river wending downtown caught a sheen as it passed under the bridge, and the haze over Lake Michigan made buildings lakeside shimmer. A white-haired man in a red-and-white-checked shirt saluted a surprised passerby as he wheeled the corner up toward the radio station. An advice columnist in a satin robe on the thirty-second floor of Chicago's second tallest building stood over her toilet and watched the water sway slightly, fore and back. A track star woke up in the shadow of the old water castle and felt his head for insects. A new mayor slammed her door.

Emerald City, 1979. Graduate school on student loans. Jazz.

Cindy

I come from alternative FM. Not the vanity of folk singers like Tom Rush or Judy Collins, of electronic rockers like Santana or Pink Floyd. I come from the gentlest voice, optimism breathed, over one acoustic guitar, in Nick Drake. I come from the trance-like intensity of Tim Buckley's sung improvisations, from the sense of dark room, dark night in Laura Nyro's diminuendos or in Leonard Cohen's rolling guitar strings beneath a baritone incantation. Jazz only in "Twisted" by Joni Mitchell, in Tim Buckley's slippery wails in "Gypsy Woman," or through the walls: my dad's big-band 78s and, on occasion, glissandos on his own clarinet.

Mainly I come from alone. Thousand Oaks, San Fernando Valley. I come from the tract house and the Lay's potato chips in a jumbo Folger's can, its red plastic lid. I come from materials made to resemble leather. A spice rack, gutted by the prior tenants, with which we "made do." A tetherball hole in the ten-foot driveway. I come from waiting in the car while Mom did errands on Saturday morning or on late, hot afternoons with the car windows down. In front of the mock-stucco post office. In the shopping-center parking lot with her pug's tongue spittling the finish on the car door as it drooled. I come from lockers where the Allman Brothers albums my boyfriend brought to school had to be inserted at a slant, from corner to far corner. From mistaking color sugar dots on paper for LSD. I come from swallowing one toke only and then pretending to be more stoned than I was, but bellying up to the Boone's Farm as it was passed about. From stealing Slickers at Sav-On. Jean Shrimpton, Lady Jane Grey. Op-art poster in the living room.

I come from wanting, from the annual broadcast of *The Wizard of Oz* certain as daylight savings, from Boiled Frozen Brick of Vegetables Late of Cardboard with Frankfurters and Beans, from the advent of Familia cereal on our shores. The incessant sun and incessant sunniness of every blond girl. The "beach," Zuma Beach, where, embarrassed by the stick figure I made in my bikini, every other girl's breasts an indictment, I watched the complicated configurations of my classmates from my box ten years deep of not belonging.

I come from a small room with a door with a large desk with a large drawer for candles and matches, with a stack of odd 45s, careful 33s, with a stereo of gray plastic with attached speakers that folded up for carrying, set on a floor once wall-to-wall blue and now splotched with wax, with Tang, walls papered with small blue and purple flowers on small green stalks. A pitch-eaved, square window.

I come from a father who came from playing the clarinet in what he called "jazz clubs," but he was an asshole and the clubs were lounges.

From a mother (alleged) who worked as a pole climber for DWP for two years after he left and who then wrenched her back one day and went on disability. From her getting migraines by sitting on Naugahyde and so switching those upholsteries for a masculine plaid soon rutted with cigarette holes, and from "your father was a sap." I come from Dacron, from stereo headphones with the telephone ringer on LOUD. Trying to prove it to them with grades.

I come from what had to be my father sleeping with his dog, figuring this out in retrospect. From his excitement over his first Shell Oil card, his scraping it along the length of my thigh to demonstrate its sharp edge and then drawing back, shook up. From Mom smoking, from my own trying to give my dolls to any kid who said they wanted them.

I come from despair at ever *getting out,* from one mulberry tree per lot, pine bark littering a patchy ground, and the neighbors at hand with their sprinklers. To the southeast, just past Universal Studios, a glittering Hollywood, Sharon Tate and TM™. Elliott Gould, private eye in a sad-sack rental. More sun and blonds. More cars. I come from driving my mother's, the Ford Fairlane, ancient then, I come from burning out its engine on the macadam of the Ventura Freeway and crying for the state I was in, no money, no resources, my mother hiding her mysterious few, my car windows rolled up against a mist, more of a spitting really, crying until the highway patrolman knocked on the fly window and although I told a boyfriend later that the patrolman had said *Well Miss Thang* he really said *License please. And registration.*

I come from circle-sitting with other kids who pulled their mothers off of floors at night, from commuting to Pierce College and then to UCLA, falling that year for a boy with sandy, curly hair, an Adam's apple and a Boston accent, poly-sci and a year on me, no beach culture to judge me by. From wanting to do well as he did well, from redeeming myself by serious purpose. From wanting his friends to be my friends, especially the woman Bobbi, wanting to *be* her—her fine features, her halo of Afro, her intactness, her skepticism, her laugh; to *do* what she could do—paint, paint big figural still lives; to understand painting as she did, to be able to talk about it in such an interesting way, to know what Clement Greenberg had written, and to know the music she listened to—jazz, jazz filling her apartment off-campus, jazz some secret code that would render me an initiate to her own hip world. From sweetening up and clamming up on the outside, trying to fit in, but also to be smart, so not forgoing wit: I wanted blend not bland, wishing I knew what she knew: choir practice, Chicago, the smell of her mother processing her hair.

And I come from that one night's outing with my boyfriend, with Bobbi and with others, to a hall in East L.A. to hear the Art Ensemble of Chicago, the length of the hall filled with clumps of gongs and horns and drums, what I took to be bongo drums and drum sets; stands holding miniature straight saxophones and outsized baritone horns;

children's trumpets and bugles and stringed uprights. Musicians wearing tribal paint, or the reeds of an African dancer, or a doctor's getup, white coat over tie and slacks, or a suit, the one in front waving a stick from which sprouted limp, fall-over strings from its tip; all of them humming, the hum growing, five of them altogether. The doctor raising a cornet and playing the first line of "When the saints," then a bleat, triangles pulled from the others' pockets tinkling underneath, then a chorus of "Devil May Care," something my dad would have denied was jazz, *his* music, but I knew it was. Their reaching the area, a good tenth mile, the bastion or installation of their instruments, and moving in deliberate fashion to their quarters, one by one notes emerging and then a melody, "The Great Pretender," springing from the doctor's trumpet, their amusement and seriousness of purpose palpable in the hall.

And then, having come, it was I, here, deciding to major in art history, reading Harold Rosenberg and thinking *what advances style,* buying new LPs of a music new to me, an I-don't- care jazz and not the pandering slop my father served up, learning and listening with Bobbi my coach, setting my Laura Nyros in the back of the crate, learning to come from anywhere but home.

{

And when I look back, this anywhere had to be Chicago, clueless as I was. Bobbi was from Chicago, her father a South-Side minister, so I thought then that she would visit if I went there for graduate school. I imagined its jazz—this jazz I was absorbing, Bobbi's, legion and homegrown, boisterous, sly—and going to Chicago's jazz clubs with my boyfriend and Bobbi. The university took me, the only one to admit me. I thought I'd learn how to look at a painting as Bobbi could look at a painting; I imagined becoming new, different, whole in Chicago. Packed, arrived, began. The university was a swipe of gray at the base of the city's canvas, and I, alone.

In hazed heat, mid-September, walking north from Chicago's Loop, telling myself I was exploring the new life, I dogged as much for tonic, gin. A sign swung beside a basement door, in, out, mirage: RECORD PALACE: J ZZ. Inside I found Acie.

Knuckles scraping rutted paint as the door opened; inside, a form on a stool blocked most of the store, and I spooked. Don't let on. Only two front bins of records beneath a low, bare bulb; I'd click through them, leave. Then—Acie's voice. Indifferent.

"They are standing on end so as the men do not have to pull them out to look at the covers. Men get distracted on account some gal has got herself big headlights or big taillights, and then they end up with some shit music for some wrong reasons." My own chest flat as rain.

He paused and I looked at him then.

"You in the market for anything special?" I saw his right eye staring off the side of his face while the left fixed on me. He was big on all sides, top included. A hairnet, the hair below the net long and limp with oil. Green stretch pants, flip-flops, a thin black U-tank taut across Sumo folds. Maybe a hundred bins were blocked by the wall of him.

I was alone, in that sea a new city is, using my flippers to feel out the surf. Most white girls would leave, I thought. Not me. My new brave life.

"Have any Featherweight Garnell?"

His left eye, squinting. "LPs or 45s?"

45s? "45s."

He moved and when he scissored a ladder and stepped up on it, quickly, I saw a mat of black hair in the pit of his arm as he reached for a shelf. Cardboard box, size of a book box and one among many, swung onto the bin in front of me.

The 45s were stacked, manifold, all by Featherweight Garnell.

{

Came the next week, and the next, and the one after that. Knowing I couldn't keep up an LP a week on my school-loan stipend.

"You again." Teddy Edwards (*Teddy's Ready!*) on the turntable beside Acie—I only knew by the cover splayed out on a bin. October, Chicago cold already, damp. In the store, still rank, smelly.

"You got a name?" Wiping his hands with a towel. Chicken skin wedged in his top teeth.

"Cindy."

"Cindy. Not many women I know name of Cindy."

"It's a white name." The store sucked the flip from the phrase.

"Oh yeah?" He raised an eyebrow and his left eye clicked. "You got a job?"

I weighed this. I'd gotten a job in the department's slide library, putting new slides into glass squares and affixing them with strips of gluey paper. "Yes."

"Nights?"

"Part-time." Sonny Rollins in a Mohawk on a cover loomed before a bridge. Maybe the alarm in my head—*don't reveal a thing*—was wrongheaded, racist. "I'm a student."

He held a hand down beside his stool, and from the shadow a dog's head, tiny, poked and lapped at the grease on his fingers. "French." He said it like a statement.

"No. Art history."

"The fine arts?"

I processed, nodded, it ended his interest. I was forgetting the hue and pitch of Bobbi's paintings, razor-edged colors abutting others. I wanted more than anything for her to call, to hear too from my boyfriend, but she didn't and I hadn't.

"You will be wanting to hear the Brothers Brecker."

What I'd heard of the Brecker Brothers was pop-jazz, a "sound for today" as my dad's was for his, so I *wasn't* wanting, but that was ungracious. I stood by the bins in front, filled mostly of cutouts and recent releases, he on his stool not four feet away, lifting the arm from the Teddy Edwards, lifting the spinning disc off its perch and then sliding the Brecker album from its cover to the turntable in a feint quick as a card shark's. For a moment I pretended to listen.

My boyfriend won't call me back. This was what I heard in my head all day. Chicago, cut off from the rest of the world by a time warp, by continental drift, by a wrinkle in space. One night when I called Bobbi she was home; "fresh milk" she'd answered, and when I balked she said cows were the way of the future, cows were going to put a canvas in every studio and make a loss leader for every activist.

"How is the new Betty Carter?" Hinting, showing off, knowing she had played in Chicago. He looked at and past me with his glass eye.

"If I want to hear a horn I listen to the Dizz." Betty Carter: belled voice, vocalese, an instrument's scat—but these were assets I thought, I'd read.

I tried another. World Saxophone Quartet? Smart adept men; baritone, tenor, alto, soprano, and a swing side of squawk:

"What the Hebrews call *shtick.*"

Muhal Richard Abrams? He'd founded the Association for the Advancement of Colored Musicians, the AACM, Chicago-based, making a magnet of Chicago, and his own piano—

"The Muhal is another purveyor of cacophony." Acie fussed with a soft vinyl square in a sleeve like a version of a single by Salvador Dali.

And now I knew what he'd think of the Art Ensemble of Chicago, of their bells, car horns, painted faces—but I asked anyway, and when he said, "Mishmash of tribalese. This all you know?", I wouldn't answer.

The door beside me clanged behind a man, a handsome face under a pageboy cap, old army-issue parka. He spread his hands and then cupped them, blowing his warm breath across his fingers.

"Afternoon, Acie."

"Wyans." Acie addressed the man but didn't look at him, bent to toss a goldfish cracker to the dog under the stool and said, to neither of us, "Ma and me can't get enough of these things."

The man began to sift through one of the front bins and I backed into the door well. I didn't care if it did feel private, I an intruder; I wanted to stay. I'd go back to California able to call Julius Hemphill *Jule;* I'd know each take of every Coltrane number ever pressed on vinyl.

The first cold day, the air cutting through the jam of the door. When I went west again, I'd be *inside.*

The dog *Ma* was hairless. "I tell you, Wyans, she picked up the mange from Roy Haynes's mother's cat?"

The customer did not look up. "That right? All the way from California?"

The night of the day I'd found Acie's I'd gone to hear Roy Haynes's band at the Jazz Lounge on Rush Street, swollen in the high of possibility, newfound city, antidote to study, slides, iconography. The beat from the discotheque upstairs from the Lounge thrummed above peeling banquettes, album covers bannering the stage below "August is Charlie Parker Month," a smattering crowd. Bobbi kissed musicians after concerts she liked and everything about Roy Haynes's set was buoying but I was afraid to kiss him, alone.

"So why do you call her *Ma?*"

The man Wyans glanced up when I asked this, moved a bin over,

Acie raising his head at me and then back, bent, to the dog. Wyans wore a green wool shirt under his parka.

"The ghost of that woman I con*dense*d in this dog. If she is around still, I want to be watching her."

"And controlling her food supply," the man said, low chuckle. "What's that you got on?"

"This?" Acie picked up the record jacket, handed it across me to the man, a double album, opening out into a fanning sleeve, with no photographs of the musicians in informal session moments, just two posed photographs of them on a bench.

"You need something, Wyans?"

"Not today."

Acie shifted on his stool. "Would you get me some Colt? Wish I could leave the store, I do."

"Your assistant tired?"

"I do not have women doing my shit for me." They meant me.

"Just your men," the man said. Acie counted four dollars and some change into the man's hand from a pleather change purse, brown and cracked, the metal of its frame corroded.

"I will take two."

The man left; through the basement window his feet crossed the street until he disappeared down the opposite sidewalk. Acie said, "Keep your eye on things for me. Your eye only." Spun off the stool, lumbering to the back of the store, clear view now of the bins, the dog

Ma looking up. She looked up again when he returned with a thin plastic cup, water dripping, and he held it under the stool while she lapped her tongue like a pimento.

The time I'd been to the big Bebop Shop, four blocks south, large, inviting, with open bins like any other record store, Ayler, AIR, Roscoe Mitchell—musicians of the avant-garde, musicians I liked, musicians Bobbi liked—were on the sound system, the jackets propped on a register easel. *Now Playing.*

"Chair for the customers." Acie, bobbing his hairnet toward a seat missing its chairback, wedged by the well of the door; I sat. Not wanting to sit, not wanting a thing but a drink.

When the man Wyans returned with the malt liquor, Acie was unwrapping the plastic on a Richie Cole release, the jacket musician looking like a high-school kid, mounds of red hair, mammoth sideburns.

"Worry this." Acie, switching the LPs on the turntable with his two-finger sleight of hand. "Wyans, this the one backed up Jefferson in May and Joel will be bringing him in on his own."

"That right?" Wyans said. He passed the brown bag and stamped flakes off his shoes. Flakes—through the dirty window dry flecks of white drifted sideways in an overcast light. Pointillist, dingy. Only October. New life I'd chosen, and cold.

Acie handed him the record jacket. "Just married that woman was in that pill-popping flick year or two back, see that?"

"Who is he?" I asked.

"I know who you mean," said Wyans. "With the figure."

"From New Jersey," Acie said to me and then to Wyans: "This one has been out awhile." Acie's ear, bent into a ragtimey piano intro, then an alto layer on "Stormy Weather." After the break, the alto got supple, spinning like the metal wand in a milkshake, the rhythm section—pink, smooth—clumping around the sax.

The man studied the jacket. "Jefferson produced it," he said.

Borderline fusion—the next cut with a bossa nova beat, bright as the Mary Tyler Moore theme; a Muzak-like guitar solo; a little flourish of scat singing. This the kind of jazz I'd thought of as my dad's, as paintings of dogs playing poker. But when I looked up, the window and its dark afternoon seemed miles away, pocked screen, silent film.

Acie coughed and I looked at him, his good eye glared, I looked away. I liked his eye on me.

Over the din in the room, the television reporter hears the mayoral flack tap on the microphone and speak. "She's on her way, ladies and gentlemen. Thank you for your patience." The cameraman standing behind him steps back again to lean against the gray partition, and Walter, bored, looks at the fingernails of his left hand against the notes on his steno pad. Only the quick shift in the room's sound alerts him. "Women and men of the press," Mommy Mayor begins, "nothing but condemnation is due the 20,000 teachers in the Chicago system who ignored the commitment of their union president and voted to strike this very morning." Walter gnaws at his thumbnail, and his cameraman yawns.

Acie

I shift so my dick does not pinch but nothing helps the shoes.

Joel, Jazz Lounge Proprietor, pretends to not notice I am spending my lettuce on his liquor. Too much history brings on the reinforcements. I can hear everything he says to his bartender Haruo and it is intended for my benefit.

"'s Aqua Velva," Haruo is saying.

"Aqua Velva's for gentiles." Joel.

"Ask him next time."

Joel grunts and I see him survey the pit to the stage, overscoping my wondrous and considerable form. Not twenty-five feet away Elvin's tenor is proving his superior strength to a microphone. Elvin and me go back some time. So do me and The Joel.

"Who's the bass?" Joel uses his hep voice on Tonto.

Haruo leans in with his arms folded on the bar and his towel up in his hand.

"Mr. Andy McCloud the Third."

"Yeah?" and even though I am reciprocating and ignoring him, too, I can tell that Joel is amused.

A light crowd Elvin has drawn, enough not to embarrass but not enough for management not to come up short. I know what The Joel pays Elvin. My feet hurt, the disco beat pounds away upstairs. All this is reminding me why generally I stay at home. It gets so stepping out is time and a half.

Elvin begins swinging into "Remembrance" and I know the end is coming. First there will be the head. The head and him taking it out too far. Time was this would not bore me.

Haruo taps me early for the tab but no, Haruo hands me over the phone and when I get off it I see him wiping down the earpiece good and then he changes bar towels.

My brother passed.

William. Man with the plan, ace with the bass, the brother the mother got to boasting on most. William with peace for the flea. Gone William. Grown. And gone.

A lady of the night and her trade are inside the door to the place on Stanton not a block from the Bowery in New York City where the taxi leaves me off. They fluff when I crowd them in the foyer and then they commotion themselves to leave. The number I do not remember, has been awhile. I stare at the buzzers for five, ten minutes and then I rattle the handle of the inside door. It pushes open without me trying. Awhile since I climbed stairs like these. Taxi man with the Lebanese noise has given me a headache but I make it to the second floor.

It does not get her up. I can tell by the dishes in the tub and the stubs in the ashtray on the table inside the door she has been sitting up all night. She is always scrubbing and watching her weight like watching alone would keep it off. Radio in the next room is down too low to hear all but a hepcat drone.

Philomena never thought me worth the trouble to keep in touch, William said. Now she looks at me hard—my midsection, my slap sandals and socks—and without getting around to asking pours me an inch and a half of gin in a coffee cup that says on it "Don't change Dicks in mid-screw" and on the bottom, under the gin, "Nixon in '72."

"You don't have luggage?"

"Yeah." And I indicate the sack to Miss Philly but I know this is not the kind of luggage she has in mind.

"You got a suit in that bag, Acie?"

"William take his with him?"

She looks to laugh. "His suits won't fit you." The cigarette she is smoking is the brown and extra-long kind fit for a Hollywood holder.

"Fast trip," she says.

Two o'clock flight, tunnel clean and green. The dark outside William's window has a brown buzz, and a garbage truck doing its thing drowns out for a spell her sucking in on her smoke. "Philly, lay it on me how."

Her big head inclines to the side and then she shakes it like a delicate woman but she is not one, and her mouth makes a O around her smoke but the smoke just stays smoke, no rings. "Heart give out. Backstage at the Deuce." Then she goes to it. "Acie, you coming in here without a suit. Don't you respect your brother? Don't you want to show up for him for once? I'll give you five dollars you go to the Goodwill, you get a suit." I wait her out, taking it in. I always had thought my brother would die at supper, choking on a chicken bone, shooting his salt pressure up.

"Masticating?"

She ignores me in pouring more gin. Her ankles are thick I see under her mumu. "What are you thinking coming in without a suit?"

"Where is he now?"

"They took him. The morgue." Then: "You're pitiful, Acie Stevenson, you can't be going without a suit."

The suit fits. Does not need a inch of giving and I look like Duke. What *is* in the Carson Pirie Scott bag are the string-up shoes, William's feet always were small. I bring the shoes out, the ones with leather so soft the leather gathers, ripples at the sole, with the slit and the sewn-on pieces butter-soft on the top of the shoes, Bennie Moten shoes. Only other time I had a pair of ground grippers come close was when I took LuLu Bradshaw to the Liberty Inn with Hodes playing. She balked fundamentally and cried and now would be my turn for it, shoed in style, waiting on William's casket.

Philomena does not seem to revise her beef. "You're going to sweat right through it, take it off now."

"Was I right?" I say.

All the rest of the time Miss Philly lags way behind the beat like she is in the quaaludes but not now. "Take it off of you, Acie Stevenson."

She can be attractive to a breast man. Her hooters are almost a foot out in front of her like bombs trussed up in cotton lace. When she leans across the table for the lighter she has to crane the breast up and over like a I beam. But she does enjoy popping the nuts. It's not that William's Philly came from better or trying to prove she is from better, she does not think herself needing to prove a thing, she is just always on me as worse. And she was on William, too, the nights out with him playing, standing, smoking wrong: his one-market market research, he said, tolerating the Philomena for more than her torpedoes, I know.

I take off the suit and the shirt and come back into the kitchen. She has got a stack of Ma's paintings by the icebox like they are garbage.

Least she got that right.

"How did you conspire yourself to lose the uptown digs," I ask and she blows out her smoke. What else has she got of William's, I wonder, outside of Ma's easel pictures.

"The jobs took a downturn."

"Are you telling me you have got work?"

"Acie, I always have work," she says, "too much work. And I always have work for assholes. Will, he—" and she pauses, not knowing yet the previousness of these remarks— "Will said, says, I am a magnet for assholes." Anger is tailor made for the Philomena, and now the shock of a dead one gives her a good occasion.

Takes three hours and buying her dinner to get out of her the history of my brother's bad ticker and she illuminates nothing in the story but her self.

The next afternoon when I wake up she is still at it. When she hangs up the phone, it is "What you ever accomplished, Acie?" I have been listening to her pule on the horn for a good half hour now and she says this not just to me. She has smoked a few although no coffee has been materializing yet. "Acie."

"Where is the coffee, Philly?"

"I said, what have you ever done to be proud for?" She has got her claws around the glass and is hanging on fast. If I do not get out from her I will flip by the funeral.

"A dump a day not count?"

"Goddamned moon pizza pie."

"You better believe it." Jerry raises his hand again and waves at the throng. On each step his belt cuts like a fart at a funeral. Goddamned last—next year, he'll go on a diet, get Maureen to let the pants out. And next year they'll get a number far away from the Roanoke-Benson Junior High School Band.

"Next year, Birdie—you and me are going to be right behind the Puglia queen and spend all day watching her ass."

Cindy

This photograph forgotten, all this time. The class-stud wannabe took it. Leaning back against the window casing to get us all in, a rim of dark belly, smooth with a fine trail of hair, between his jeans and his shirt. Nikon in hand like a highball. Thinking about it now, coming across it in papers from that semester, the first, a month into it maybe, I remember his attitude. The slide-library workers, boss, professor—them, too.

Did they all want a drink? I thought everyone did then. The one in a cashmere cardigan, polished teeth. The next one, squinting, her dissertation on the symbolist Schwabe. The one who was Finland-obsessed, her name—Brenda. Then my boss and whose office it was, slides stacked about her on the long wooden tables where I worked, fingers cramped. She looks away in the photo, hair in a dark swab at her neck. The one who lived with a brain surgeon, thumb at his lip, a volume on rococo chairs beside him. The girl Lydia, soigné, trim like a doll, and the one with the fiancé in Paris. Apart, looking pained, thin hair escaping thin braid, thin shirt half out of my jeans, pale skin: me. Then Professor Bartel, stomach bulging at his hips like a Russian stacking doll's.

U of C Art History All Stars, someone had written on the base of the photo, *To Cindy Kinney.*

How do I remember their names? In classes and out, studying them, rattled by the scale of their lives: $300 skirts, purses from Italy, once I overheard one say she'd just come back from London. The clumps of rich students at UCLA had been dispersed in the crowds, ignored by my boyfriend and his friends, Bobbi, therefore me; and yet, here, they prevailed, groomed, hermetic. To no art historian, to none of the two dozen MA students vying for shots at PhDs, would I have revealed the still slovenliness of my mother's house.

I remember being in the picture by accident. Soon after I found Acie's, stopping by on a Friday for my paycheck. From the hall I saw students lining up in the glass-walled office, antic and soundless through the glass at once; antic enough to deter me but need for my check won out. My boss's nails were peaked and red on the envelope she held out to me, palm down. "Here. You stand here." Her English manifest through her Yugoslavian accent by gesturing to the spot.

The others still clowning. I escaping their notice. And then, with the photographer arcing, aiming, Professor Bartel rose from Simone's chair, standing, unsmiling, beside me.

Some days I hadn't spoken except to say *thank you* at Valois: See Your Food. In the used bookstore on Fifty-seventh Street, I overheard a

porkpied patron urging Spinoza on a girl and, as I left the store, con-
cert notices rippling on a plywood fence flapped at my sleeve.

Dorm like a grain chute in the Gothic set of the university. I bought
a hotplate, pan, frozen peas.

In the slide library I slipped the cardboard casing from the slide;
masked the image, with silver tape, covering the thumb and the bind-
ing where the book had lain on the copy stand; then, with the sand-
wich of glass squares, I wet a paper strip on the porcelain waterwheel
and burnished the edges so the slide would drop smoothly from the
carousel into the projector. The strip was too wet and it pocked and
burred at the cattlebone folder.

Professor Bartel's class was in a stark white box, the projector's whirr
muted in its booth, students sprinkling the steep, tiered seats.

A small light on the podium shadowed his features from below, he
cuing an audiotape and stepping into the darkness of the wall beside
the screen; there a man in a conical hat overran the edge, his black
and white legs creased like flippers. We were in Zurich, at the Cabaret
Voltaire, 1916; Hans Arp was performing before us his *Verses without
words*. The nonce syllables rolled from the speakers and set on impas-
sive faces like dogs.

Seats creaking in the shifting around me; the girl beside me
uncrossed and recrossed her legs. How could they be bored? The

nonsense, then the German—furious sonic clusters bounding from speakers, crackling, patterned. Me, the performance woke. It was then that I knew I had tried to graft art like a tree, and that my trunk wouldn't take. The slides put me to sleep but this gibberish—*the sound of it!*—was the bark that was taking, rooting, springing with shoots.

Back then, half shut down, alone, I didn't know to stop it, to get off the train, untie the graft, drop out of art history and into the music. Film ending, still images again, slides—Dada posters, Schwitters's Merzbau—and I stayed.

Halloween and an all-come party. Fussiness to the apartment, Raphael reproduction in the john. My colleagues in costume as Leda, a Ray-o-Gram, the dead Marat. Captain Frans Banning Cocq from *The Night Watch*. One wore a circle of painted industrial felt representing a Greek vase. I came as Sun Ra in tin foil and explained, over and over—each colleague curious but cool as a rock until the room folded, ribbon candy, in the light.

Cool dark like spit on the street.

And then—before the music had fizzed in my blood like the worm in Mezcal, before Acie said one day I'd "grown ears"—I drank my first fifth in one sitting.

{

And this scared me, alone, like Mom, I'd drunk a fifth without blinking, the city a dark wall between me and my world. The next night I'd go out, be around people, not drink alone, hear music. A $5 loft show on Hubbard, musicians that would draw a younger crowd, no bar. So I went.

On the speakers was that Ornette Coleman tune, "Lonely Woman," the one he did on *The Shape of Jazz to Come,* but it was Lester Bowie's version, Lester and Julius Hemphill and Cecil McBee and Lester's brother Joseph, slow minor notes, scary edge to the downdraft of the second melodic phrase, the space between these notes a whole city skyline at night, out the high windows of the loft, Mwata Bowden's ensemble riffing scales and a child doing a Frankenstein lope toward his mother. Incense drifting from across the room, blond wood floors and brick walls painted white, bright, a large floorcloth up front demarcating the stage, a semicircle of folding chairs and heat scant. A woman regal in a tall headdress surveyed the room from beside the stage, laughing at something the hand-drummer said as he set a string of handbells in place.

I'd treated the hangover with shooters, no food. I felt good. Woozy good.

"You have to keep in mind he didn't want to go in that direction." From behind me. "He'd seen too many get chewed up by what they got *fixed up with,* y'know what I'm saying? And that was his gift, foresight, a remarkable foresight. He had big ears, too, that man, big ears."

Another voice, younger: "I hear Kalaparusha was flying on Saturday," pause. "Did you go down for the big band?"

The conversation lifted over the scales in snippets: "*that* cat. Oh yeah I know" and "throw any key at him, a *griot*"—then, close to my ear; I turned. "Hi. Harnett Mtukufu," few years older and he was smooth, smooth and sleek, kufi and wire-rims, a reporter's pad, holding one hand in a C for a handshake I didn't know. "This is my friend Don Recusa. I'm interviewing Don for *Down Beat.*"

The pianist wore a serape and looked out beyond my right shoulder, silent. Harnett Mtukufu not noticing, using a low voice to him; Recusa, unwavering, watching the musicians, and I turned back, toward the stage. "Have you heard Mwata before?" Harnett again, leaning over, slipping the notepad into his jacket like a glove. He had a broad, symmetrical nose, a jaw muscle that beat in his cheek. Cool density of jeans on my legs.

Mwata Bowden started the set with a long soprano sigh. It pierced the crowd into stillness; a little girl covered her ears, looked up. The sigh became noodling, a sign for percussion, and a clipped, syncopated roll seemingly unrelated to the saxophone built to a voracious thrum, until a trombone took over the noodling idea and the drummer switched to the cymbals while the soprano used its lowest register for a kind of parody of a ballad.

The beat threw me, but not the sound: the brain, jumping. The interplay turned on a dime. Music that seemed awkward recorded was here an environment, a structure, a surround wide-open as the lake, and something in the banter and the braying made me forget about myself. No longer a body in a chair in a loft as bright as Christmas, no longer the figure that, despite others' neglect, wouldn't erase. I wasn't Bobbi or my boyfriend's castoff, I wasn't the student straining to care, the oddball without a life that staked claims. The time signatures shifted; the clusters of notes knotted up like an onslaught of thoughts. Nothing else did this but alcohol.

It was Bobbi's music. This was something my dad could never have gotten, despite his playing Benny Goodman on an odd night or two, plopping a cocktail onion in his glass. For him, the music meant a lifestyle: women with cigarettes in bouffants, natty ties, big sedans. His *cool combos* were just the means of honing in on the dames he craved, *cooler* than the insurance he sold by day.

After each solo a few people applauded as audiences did with bebop. Silence suddenly, and Mwata Bowden introduced the musicians, and then said, "The music isn't about clapping." The next number: a unison march, a rock path pebbling away, its elements becoming sand

and vegetation dense and cacophonous. Suddenly quiet, clearing, Mwata soaring alone on oboe now, leaving broken terrain for sky. I was that bird, too, thrilling at the peak, coasting. Surge. Then silence.

"Thanks be to Allah." Forty, fifty minutes it had been—still early, families on a school night—the audience preparing to disembark the craft. Headdress woman going toward the musicians, hum building and breaking off from the speakers, percussionist turning a long drum on its side.

"Catch you later:" Recusa. Harnett Mtukufu at his arm, saying something to him. Recusa shrugging as he left.

No one else in the crowd seemed to acknowledge Harnett Mtukufu, *Down Beat* reporter. He buttoned his old-man overcoat, adjusted his wire-rim frames.

"It's still early," he said. "Where are you off to, girl?"

Apprehension. "South Side."

"Oh yeah?"

"Well, Hyde Park."

Dead giveaway. "You study? What do you study, girl?"

"Art. Art history."

Harnett Mtukufu took this in, looking at me straight on, and then looked away, toward the door, thought stirring his face like a spoon. I didn't want him to smell the whiskey so I held my breath.

"Have you had supper? Yesterday I had a colonic and I've been hungry ever since."

A colonic was what? I didn't eat out, it was bad enough I was blow-ing this money on sets, drinking, LPs, but I needed to know someone besides students, to go out, have a drink, curiosity. An attractive man and he knew Don Recusa. Ornette didn't give it words, "Lonely Woman," just notes. A measure, let alone a minute, could hold a lot of notes, and it was up to me to hear them. But how could anyone hear when I couldn't describe it later, when no one was around to hear it?

Supper. Imagining the click-shoop of opening a Tecate, lime burn-ing my lips. "Okay." Independence, the drug.

Outside, rain freezing on the pavement, on the cement staircase to Michigan Avenue, in the air around us. Standing I felt the Jack Daniel's surge, bright hunger cutting in. "—a macrobiotic place on Seventy-fifth," Harnett was saying, South Side, further than the uni-versity, past its ribbon of traffic that whites called the DMZ. What could happen? Cold, wet. "It's okay, girl, I've got wheels. I'll drop you after. Just parked over the bridge."

The *Hideaway* bar, home of swing jams, was back down the stairs to Hubbard Street. A drink there, he and his wire-rims, no car riding, no red light flashing, or we could go to the down-market sliders bar where happy hours filled with commodities traders, happy hour now long gone. He, looking again, laughing. "I won't bite." What my boy-friend would say, and how he said it: laughing, *I won't bite.*

Volvo, green slick in the wet on Lake Street. He keyed it on, idled it, took a rag to the windows, I surveying the papers clotting the backseat, the empty slot under the dash for a tape player, the scuzz. Examining, in a detached way, attraction: *maybe* was the upshot, in the wooze. Harnett climbed in and took off his gloves, flicked water off his eyebrow with the back of his thumb, touched the wheel. "This mother is *cold*."

No sparkly Lake Shore Drive along the lake. He took Michigan Avenue; south of downtown buildings thinned and the streets darkened, each boarded brownstone abutting another in rubble. Martin Luther King Boulevard. Occasionally a corner light, a grill discernible three feet in, a fellow wending his way from the light with a small paper sack. The road was slick, Harnett focused, a sudden red light and small skid. I'd give it a whirl, pulled the bottle from my pocket, offered it.

"You drink, girl?" His hands on the wheel. "I'm off it for the meantime. Got my *temple* fucked up, so I'm taking a vacation." Swallow, the warm into my throat and down, drained. Fear too racist to admit to had cleared my head.

If I wasn't in school, for a while they might think I was just cutting class. Or traveling.

He passed Fifty-fifth Street, Sixtieth, the lefts that would take us to Hyde Park. Turned on Seventy-first, passed the long dark blocks of a cemetery until the streets lit again, rubble now beside storefront beside brownstone boarded upstairs, lit downstairs: a mix. Up a side street and then another, dark, Harnett stopped. Alert, I climbed out of the car, righted myself, *hungry,* smash of a bottle a block away, silence, and then Harnett opened an unmarked door and light and noise slammed me.

A restaurant hung with kente cloth, and soup came chunky with beans but no wine, no beer, no screwdrivers or margaritas on the menu, other tables had brought their own. I wavered in assurance and then grabbed my hunger and ate with it. Harnett, himself eating with keen absorption.

What was he, why did I care? If I could sate the craving like a boy, if I could just screw and let live, not entangle, not pine away later.

His napkin at his mouth, a fastidious wiping. "So how long have you been on the Chicago scene?"

"A couple of months."

"Studying art? Paintings and whatnot?"

"Mostly—"

"Lot of art going down in Chicago. You'll have to meet some of those people, girl, lots of professional artists here. And galleries—"

"I've made the rounds a bit," I said.

His fork paused; now he swallowed inadvertently. "You know some collectors?"

"Sure," I lied. Collectors of the boxes of Joseph Cornell had invited the whole program to their house for wine, their affability shaming my hanging-back but still I didn't utter a word, following my classmates about the house like a sheep.

"Have you heard my show?"

I hadn't.

"It's on KLB, I just got the Sunday morning slot—before that it was Tuesdays and Thursdays, midnight to 5 a.m. That's why my system is so messed up—burned out from the boneyard shift."

"Really. And you write, too?"

He turned the lid up on the teapot, gestured to the waitress. "Some on-air and off-air interviews and reviews for *Down Beat* and *The Reader.*" He said this too carefully to be playing it down. "You know, Cindy Kinney, I'm a Rumsey—" I hearing *I'm a Pepper,* a commercial, "my mother was a Rumsey from Detroit—before I changed my name to Mtukufu. Means 'His Excellency' in Swahili."

Something so presentational, so impersonal, in his rambling, a familiar feeling: *no room here for me.* Not necessarily meaning he wouldn't want sex—or, perhaps especially, that I wouldn't. I did.

One night, before Christmas, I maybe four, five: my dad's clarinet in the yard. It woke me; freezing at the window, then, I looked at his frame on the small patch of lawn by the street. Some ballad, minor scale—the kind of thing he never usually played, never listened to unless it was orchestrated to the hilt—the sadness of this, the loneliness of him, making the ranting and railing and the tornado of him a thing apart.

Harnett Mtukufu pulled up to the dorm, squinted at the hotel next to it, hesitated, I hesitated, then sober and thinking, suddenly, I opened the door.

"Hey, I'm in the front line for invitations with my radio gig. If you've got a card I'll let you know my play list, cue you on the underground, if you like the AACM and whatnot. I've been around this scene my whole life." Then he put his hand on my knee and his mouth in my hair. Brown swirl of his shirt. In my room we'd have a drink.

The contractor pulls up to the client's door with his boy in tow, discovers the child has found some chocolate, and looks in vain for Kleenex, paper, anything to wet and wipe. Then he begins to lick his son, methodically, up one cheek, chin, up the other. A palm to his mouth. The boy is laughing. Downtown, on the fourteenth floor of Marina Towers, a broker in a long down coat locks her door behind her and sprints to catch the elevator's open door. In a Humboldt Park apartment, a man in a Bears cap frying chorizo stops for a moment to sing a phrase along with Eddie Colón. He twirls the spoon like a top on his hand. The broker steps into Riccardo's and waves a hand at the coat check: "I'm keeping it tonight, sugar." Near north, in the shadow of Mies, the contractor unrolls the sketches on a coffee table and keeps one eye on his son.

Acie

Upon my return to Chicago Bowtie is there to pick me up. Five o'clock and already dark as Bosco. The night I transported my self to New York I told him to stay put, just pick me up when I return, and he in that regalia of his comes down the corridor after I sit awhile at the gate, reading about the Captain and Tennille in a *People* a stewardess left. The door on Bowtie's white-boy foreign car is stuck in the sleeting that is froze in the lock and I got to pound it to get a crack.

He breaks out the WD-40 for his steering post and the Colt 45 malt liquor for me, and then he rolls onto the Kennedy Expressway with the city laid out on either side. The blowhard Dick Gibson (*Hardly a Dick* what Bowtie calls him) introduces a Cab Calloway in the radio glowworm.

I always liked cars at night, even with Bowtie, even when he was a foot long and putting a tear on the backseat with his screaming in the days before his mother left me. Even with him knee-high, his snot running down the side of a cloth we got him for his sniveling. Now at a quarter century he still got the edgy look where you *know* there is still snivel.

"Jazz Fair tomorrow," he says. He works at my competition at the

Bebop Shop on account his mother raised a hustler. The so-called Jazz Fair is nothing but a few white folks selling off their LPs in a school lobby and the same old show movies of the Duke rolling in the room to the side. Every year his boss has been onto me to take part in this all-city Jazz Fair but I have short enough goodwill without testing it on some gators at a card table in some school-side lunchroom.

The mother raised the hustler, but the grandmother on the father's side cemented the pretension, I admit to it. Combination makes him hard to bear.

The Calloway runs so up-tempo it could give me a headache. Bowtie looks my way and then back at the expressway. "How was it?" he says. Behind his head cars blur from his habit of passing on the right.

What I flash on is the service but there is no conversation in it.

"It was a funeral." His face hangdogs so I think to try.

"Philly can beat the gums. You remember when your uncle played The Joel's—" Bowtie nods but I know he does not because he was high the whole year that year. "She put that cologne on your wallet so your money smell sweet. And you did not even know yet what your money could buy." I do not doubt he *did*.

Highway at night makes a city look good. Lights in the sprawl are like sequins on a woman of abundance. Up ahead Walter Payton has himself a big picture side of a building. "Fucking do not even interest a woman like that."

"How would *you* know?" Bowtie says, sly for him.

And then we get the shock, a slamming of a roar behind and it gives us a jolt, tornado on our tail. Shock comes too fast for thinking, but that trouble attractor Bowtie's nerves take the wheel to the right. His head turns back, front. He stares in the rearview. I do not rotate good so I open the window and maneuver into the side mirror and there is a creamy Cadillac sitting right on Bowtie's toy car.

The driver and the passenger is black but that is all I can see. The Cadillac makes its noise again and a bid for our backseat.

"Shit!" Bowtie looks back and forth from vista to mirror and then, "Shit!"

The offspring has the eyes of someone who does not get much trouble. "Get your seat belt on!" he says. "You—" and then he is back on the mirror. The quick and the consideration come from my genes but the impatient is from his ma's.

No business this car has in the left lane but the boy takes it there now. The Cadillac pulls in behind us again. Middle lane, Bowtie got his foot to the floor and his glasses steaming in his own salt sweat. The city of Chicago drums its own beat: Addison, Belmont, Diversey. Road lights on a fast clip.

Bowtie may be edgy but he can also be quick, too, and of a sudden he is on the right lane and we are shot off the expressway early. I hear the squeal of the predator on the road we left. Bowtie brakes on the ramp and his tin car with us in it spills out onto North Avenue, heading west. A voice, "I'll never smile again," high and sweet, floats of a sudden from the radio. Out of nowhere I am hearing: *Son of mine is good for nothing.*

Bowtie twitches when he scares. "Jesus," he says and then again, "Jesus."

I do not know whether to baste him or box him but I select the former. "I am going to kill you, then I am going to make another looks just like you only better. If you know the cats—do not give me your jive. If regardless they were agents or your best bloods, if they are at you for a reason you are a full fool. What in—" He has the pitiful look about him. "No, you keep to yourself the real deal. Just keep it out from me."

Then he lays back in an unnatural way, trick he picked up from his equally lowlife mother. And he *knows* it gets into me. "Sorry, Acie. Not to worry." Past the donut shop, left, left, and on to Milwaukee Avenue he goes. Bric-a-brac lots, brick piles. The offspring cool at the wheel but quiet.

"That's the Tommy Dorsey Orchestra with Connie Haines." Radio and Hardly a Dick talk like nothing happening. Up close Chicago is not so appealing.

Bowtie shakes his head and the little hat on it and looks up at me eager as a dog. "Every city's got one," he says thinking I care to listen.

"What!" My blood has rushed. Burn me just try, small fry, Bow tie.

"An old white man with a good collection."

The women have them and then ever after just try to recognize them. Bowtie: the heir.

Joe Henderson has the best tongue in the business. He enunciates clear as glass. I tell Bowtie's boss this one day when he comes by as he does to see if I am cutting into his business. I say this about Joe's enunciation, and a bagman crowding Bowtie's boss at the bins starts then lambasting "the virgin." I can not make hide nor hair and then he says "and Mary went" and I clarify he thought I meant *an*nunciate. *E*nunciating not *an*nunciating I say to him but the gentleman is so balled up he just starts repeating "Joe-*Hen*der" like "yo *ma*ma" so I and Bowtie's boss steer him out.

This is what I have been saying. You can not tell in advance of calamity. A white girl comes in who may be for all I know one of the many loco ladies out there (a legion I have seen and more than my share), hair like butter on stringy noodles, looking for something she will not say. She may be harmless enough but she sends out a panoply of blewy signals. Ali from the hotel upstairs I know has designs on the cashbox, but there is always one that do, and the dog Ma may not be Ali but she is loud. Back when we delivered to hotels, when the artists in town for their gigs needed a new long-play, Buzzy and later Bowtie when he ran for me had some scrapes, too. You got over forty white persons still in keeping by those race-thinners in Iran, a peanut farmer the chief sweet talker for the capitalist side.

And then you got a brother William dead.

The funeral has just been this morning and tonight Bowtie and me get run off the road. Philly rings up to say did I get to Chicago all right and by the by, while out for a drink her place was looted. I see before my eyes her drum-case bras lined up like trash bags. It comes on me that bees are buzzing around the relations and the dread it makes for me is a motivator to lock my own windows. I have stayed out of trouble for fifty-nine years and I am not interested in taking the plunge now.

Here is an example. Last week I went to the early show for the movie with Barbarella and that white glamour boy out of *The Sting* and the headshrinker that shrinks the white doctors imperializing Koreans on TV. Glamour boy is a cereal cowboy they got up in Christmas tree lights to sell cereal but he tells them they can eat shit and goes off to free a horse because in Hollywood being white they like horse freeing. Point until then is he was broke when he was a display piece like a horse is broke. Then he comes into some action. But the action as he said in this movie is not about TV. There is action in here so private no one can hear shit from the middle of it.

I find the shop-proprietor pistol and strap it under my shorts. I double-lock the front gate and I am propping in position the corner mirrors so as I can see the bounce from the back. Somewhere I have put the laser Bowtie got me off the street few years back and I have ideas but they will wait until the morning. I string out the phone line and put the phone by the bed and then I sleep like a baby.

In the middle of the night the Baggie gets cold. I feel the bag with my hands and try to go up on my knees holding the bottom of the bag and the top of it close to my nuts as I liberate the dick. A siren on State Street *wa-wa*s away. Outside the back window of the crib I can see the glint of the streetlight beyond the bramble lot and the hotel, and I crack the pane and toss my gold. A couple of sprinkles blow back on my chest hairs and ice up in the air streaming in.

Would not be me wanting to freeze.

In the dark I look for my knits and shoes. About 3 a.m. I am finding the laser from when Bowtie thought I needed a hobby besides the trim. By 3:30 I got it replacing the Mongo box on the back wall and in the deep dark of 5 I got it aimed to loop each mirror on the four corners and connect itself up with itself, where all I need is a light cell battery in order to trigger my own siren when the door opens and the light loop breaks. I got just the music on the reel-to-reel and a better alarm there is not.

This is the kind of cagey action at which I am the master. By 5:30 the phone ringing again and Miss Philly has other actions in mind. She has been up, too.

"Acie Stevenson, I am giving you the opportunity to return the hospitality. I am flying in."

The TV is perched on the bed stand next to the wall shrine, and now it is saying that the mayor will move into Cabrini Green and go to work in her limousine. Glancing up, the man sees the mayor woman with yellow hair standing in front of the black projects with microphones, and then he focuses again on the two bowls before him on the dresser. He can't get what fish there is to look like much in the thin broth. Now is an ad for a car dealership. The man cuts fronds of Chinese parsley into the soup with children's scissors, and stirs the bowls with the blades until they cloud. A picture of President Park Chung Hee and the letters "KCIA" hang behind the newscaster.

His wife, from the bed, curses.

"Ta destoyo."

Cindy

{

The next day, Acie withstanding my request for Abbie Lincoln's "People in Me," her plinky-plonky voice resounding over his grimaces. The little dog, Ma, wagging his tail excitedly, looking at me as I watched Acie, me grinning, wagging my shoulders. I did a little spin and knew Acie's annoyance was more for show than blow. "Acie!" I said. "What's not to like?"

Another day.

> . . . 'til April in Paris.
> *Whom can I run to?*
> *What did you mean to—*
> *what have you done to my heart?*

And then the needle at the end of the record side made a ticking sound.

"You been taken to Paris?" Acie didn't look around at me—shuffling LPs in near the back of the room—but when I shook my head he said, "That is a shame. A lot of musicians like to go to Paris."

As usual, the obvious when it came to educating me. "I know." He fixed on some cellophane wrapping, slit and pulled it from the cardboard cover, coming forward, the-dog-Ma following him, looking up at him, panting.

"What happened to your eye, Acie?"

"For example, this novelty number. You might think it originated in Paris but the Club Sudan that planted its seeds was uptown New York. You been taken to New York?" He was at the turntable, putting the LP on it, cueing. Tarzan drums, a portentous flute in the foreground.

"You got Sabu, Potato, Jose, and they are only the congas. Evil Quintero, Evil comes in—there—on the tree log. That is Herbie Mann, the flute. You tell who are the home patriots on rhythm?"

"What happened to your eye, Acie?"

"Which piece of information is going to get you your college diploma."

"I'm not *studying* music, Acie."

"Music is not a fine art?"

"Visual art, I'm studying *visual* art."

He was bent over the-dog-Ma, even arguing he was diffident. "Then what are you doing in the Record Palace bending your ears, Sally, instead of tuning your eyeballs?"

"Cindy."

"Who are the Americans comprising the rhythm section here?"

What *was* I doing. The last three loan statements spread out, the Colt 45 can to one side, a little unstable on the wall-to-wall, the plastic shade on the plastic lamp positioned over my notebook and the bills and the tuition statement and the bank statement. Bobbi once had said she'd go to graduate school to live on borrowed money awhile longer but I wasn't getting it to work, my slide-library check didn't even keep me in beer. Restless, all I wanted was to leave—leave the dorm room, leave the classroom, leave Acie's, leave bed with Harnett. But where to go—numbers blurring like features, no face.

I remember that blur. And then the phone ringing, Harnett.

Dressed. Up. In a dress, combed, painted with brows and lashes and lips. In the moment the owner greeted us, lit doorway of Pierrot ("Mr. Mtukufu!"), in his deference with Harnett's worn overcoat, it was exhilarating, worth it. The dining room clean, uncluttered, elegant, the light light but not bright, Harnett and his color conspicuous among the older patrons, the traders, the elderly, the blond, dishy wives. Plates at our table featuring iconography even, the harlequin Pierrot.

"It's a private restaurant, you have to be a member." Boasting, then dipping his kufi and his head, briefly, prayer-like, accepting the short list of dinner alternatives, passing the wine list to me. Studying his menu.

Then: "You know, at the end of the sixties, it was Roscoe Mitchell and Malachi Favors—there was this bass player, too, pupil of Wilbur Ware's named Charles Clark—"

"Just a minute," I said.

I'd stared at the wine list without reading a word. Now I found the cheapest red for the aproned waiter, anticipated it then, watching Harnett's mouth again moving, trying to tune him in, a radar wavering, honing in, the cone of it sketchy on the dial. Just turn down the edifying, fella. Then something in him sensed this, stopped.

"How's the art business?"

And as I thought to say *my heart's not in it,* Harnett, again: "You know girl, I don't even know what particular period you are studying."

My own boast, then, delivered in kind. Take this. "Right now, some German painters—the *die Brücke* group." And, oddly, this registered with him. Sudden blip, and then the waiter swooped back with the bottle, showing me the front of it, static, until I looked up at the waiter's puffy face, what next, and he cut a circle in the top foil and began to twist the corkscrew. I anticipating it in my mouth, on my throat, then looking back at Harnett who now was unruffled, unsurprised, so that I thought I'd invented his response. But a hesitancy when he spoke again.

"So what do you think of the art *here?*" he asked. The waiter waited as I tasted, Harnett covered the top of his glass as the waiter poured mine, I sipped again. Nodded. Fortifying. The room glowed, above the tables along the opposite wall five framed paintings, three sort of cubist, a central group of objects bisected and collected, each at a different angle, like early Picassos, or like Juan Gris, this much anyone could tell. An acrylic sheen to them that made them tinny. In the others, heavily outlined figures, one with a Pierrot staring out directly, mournfully, beside a slutty woman baring her breast on a ladder. A circus caravan.

"Those two figural ones are kind of interesting," looking still at the paintings but drinking from the glass, warming up.

Like paintings by the German artist, Max Beckmann, one of the painters we'd been studying in Professor Bartel's class; the Art Institute had one of Beckmann's self-portraits, he elegant in a tuxedo, looking wary and weary, on a kind of gangplank or grand staircase hard to say which, the colors deep, the black of the tuxedo engulfing except for his hands, each as big as his head, cuffed white. One of the first artists whose work I had been shown by Bobbi, pages in a book spread to the three panels of "Departure," the center one a king, woman, and child, spirited on a boat by someone masked.

"They look like Max Beckmann's," for if Harnett would quiet in my own display of knowledge then I would continue; intimidate; I would give him some of his own know-it-all medicine.

For the second time, he seemed shook, alerted, a dip in his sureness. It worked. And then I felt his knee against mine.

I finished the wine. He signed the check. He held the door of his car and glanced across at me, bright but quiet, oddly quiet, for Harnett. Still, as the quartet set up in the university chapel, he began to edify me again, and in the middle of a lesson on Albert Ayler's soprano saxophone, someone tapped Harnett on the shoulder, said something close to his ear, and he acted as if the need to mollify was his. "I'll be right back, won't be long," he said, leaning to me, "Remember where we were."

The chapel stone and cold, arched windows bearing cast-iron joints. Warm from the wine but chilling fast, my coat, my hat, my scarf I kept on, one musician setting up turning to another and smiling as he gestured, shivering, a self-hug. Harnett slid back in the pew.

"Let's move down—that's Johnson." He indicated a doughy man in a knit shirt huddled over a *Sun-Times*.

Obliged, moved away, took the bait. "Who's Johnson?"

"Herb Johnson—you've read him. *Down Beat, Tribune*. He always comes out for the out-of-towners' gigs." Harnett unbuttoned his coat. "You ever heard Kalaparusha Maurice McIntyre? He used to play with J.B. Hutto and Little Milton, you know that?" Harnett pointing out the local notables, musicians, men in the business—they were all men—Harnett back to his usual self now, I not ungrateful for his lessons, wanting intimacy, though, in the tone. *A little tenderness*, I thought, *just try*.

"Harnett, you're a font—"

He smiled, leaned away, "Shit, you're my white-girl project."

"Do you know that basement record store on State?" I asked. "Run by this fellow Acie?"

For a moment Harnett's face mimed incredulity. And then the room stilled, and his face turned toward the stage, he leaning sideways toward me and whispering. "Sure, all the old-timers go there. That cat's a character." Tall, courtly figure with a tenor sax ("Billy Harper," Harnett whispered, nodding) looked at his musicians, nodded. "It is *cold!*" Then silence, prayer, said "priestess" into the mike then stepped back, pianist beginning a simple, lyrical line repeated, building, like a canon.

Dah. Dah da-da dah da-dah. Dah da-da dah da-dah. Dah dah *dum* dah dah C run C *Dah.* Repeat. The drum—with a hi-hat skimming—joining, then the sax and trumpet and bass, in a unison line, repeating the figure. They veered into grace notes, embellishing the theme, then a long trumpet trill signaled them *out*—Billy Harper picking up the trill, the five of them *gone*.

Gone, later, more wine, Harnett's lobe in my teeth, his working his hand beneath my zipper, the sharp smell of him, grass and loam, his eyes shut. Blurred so close, the face not a full one but its parts, and then not sight and sound but skin.

And later still, waking to find Harnett alert and watching me, while keeping a beat on the mattress with his big toe. Divided he was, between Good Boyfriend Behavior and antsiness, always. "What are you thinking?" I asked.

"Tell me about these collectors you know, girl. They collect what you study? Europeans?"

This sat me up. "Why do you care?"

"Just asking. Some collectors I may know, too." His attention split, his head turning.

Embarrassed—I didn't really know any—and curious, I deflected. "Why, who do you know?"

He slid onto his back, his arm at my hip like an electrified prod. "Quite a number, owner of Pierrot, for example." His eyes, closing. "Go back to sleep."

From the el stop at Randolph I walked over the river to Acie's. Cold, bone cold, buildings emitting chutes of high, white steam. Cars turning beside the river on Wacker Drive quickly, each isolate under the gray sky. Woman whose legs looked bare, pumps, down coat, blond hair and briefcase swinging, running to make the light. In the cold, a man without gloves on the bridge did a scale on a saxophone, sliding then into a chorus of "Starlight," standing over an open case. I looked away, cold, tried to focus on the Wrigley Building's spire. Bus and a matron's scowl.

Record Palace was warm. I made sure the door was fully latched behind me and took a moment to inhale the heat and Joe Williams swing, *Live at the Century Plaza*. "Show me where to scratch, baby, show me where it's at." Acie fave rave.

"Sadie." Acie coming from the back, toward his stool. "Afternoon."

Learning Chicago afternoons in winter were just evenings. "It's Cindy." His razor look.

"Remembering shit is not my bag."

I handed him his own bottle, opened mine. "Can I look behind?" I asked, not the first time, today not because I was looking for anything in the open stock but because it would be even warmer away from the door. Big show of sucking in his gut to let me pass in the aisle but his gut didn't really move and I squeezed by, carefully indifferent. Bins he usually blocked stretched before me like Mecca. Settling on the spare horn-cum-fusion of Miles Davis. *Acie won't approve. Fuck him.* I took a long sip, flipping the jackets.

He was distracted, attending to some papers and envelopes in front of him, not looking up. "Where *you* been? Thought you was leaving town for the winter."

"I was here the other day but you weren't." The gate had been pulled across the door on a day snow came down in sheets.

Squinting his good eye, trying to turn toward me, his heft preventing. "Had things to attend to." Joe Williams half spoke *good lowdown lovin', baby,* Acie's papers rustled.

"Lawyers make quite an investment in themselves."

Another pause. "My aunt Chappy," Acie again, "—did I ever tell you about my aunt Chappy? She one of those that has got religion so bad the only way she can get her thing diddled is to go to the doctor. She took her self to the doctor every week once she understood he was flat-out more satisfying than the lawyer she had used to hound. 'Course she had served every family member before medicine took its hold."

He *had* told me about his aunt Chappy, except last time her name had been Hettie and she was his godmother. I was tired of his racy pontificating. The only reason he took this tack week after week was to test me. Did I think that if I weren't white—

Suddenly picturing the other graduate students and their purposeful organization. I drank, caught my sleeve on the bin, mopped the drops from the record-sleeve ends. He not paying attention, relief. The door in front of Acie opened and two kids came in, polite, shivering. "You want to buy some candy?" One, with a bag.

"Do I look like I am buying what you are selling?" Acie had a snort for occasions like these but this time didn't use it. "What you got?"

Other students with families, people looking after them, investing in their progress. Bonnard interiors versus Hopper. Side B had finished on *Live at the Century Plaza,* and the needle was making the *stip, stip* sound in the groove Acie called the *eccentric.*

The boys left, squabbling over the bills, Acie opening one wrapper, regarding me.

"Do not discount *Sketches of Spain,*" he said. I did. Fifties artwork, Miles-Davis-&-strings LP.

"I don't like it," I said, flipping past it.

He turned toward me so as not to crane and I knew he was staring.

I met his gaze for a moment and then moved on to the South African tenor, Johnny Dyani. "Too fat and clumsy," I said. "Orchestras and big bands are like turning a tank." Acie cleared his throat, spit into the cup beside the turntable, stared.

"Here. Let me show you something." He hoisted off his stool, gestured for me to take his hand. What the—I knew without thinking that if I demurred, the breach would be large. Etiquette. Prop the bottle in the bin first. I didn't, took it with. Acie pretended not to notice my hesitation and led me toward the beaded curtain at the back of the store.

He drew it back for me. "This is my setup." I could make out a dark room with high basement windows along the back wall. Cement for floor, cement for walls, open struts, wires and pipes on the ceiling. Stained American flag, poster of Farah Fawcett on the right wall, a skeezy double mattress on the floor beneath them. A refrigerator and sink, pocked, grimy, against the wall of what seemed to be a closet but became, as my eyes adjusted, a toilet stall.

I smelled him beside me.

Let go of his hand. I was being given the house tour, was all. This seemed a reasonable guess; I said, "Nice! Great place." Acie, smiling, pausing, I concentrating on being breezy, relaxed, turning back toward the store. Nonchalant, wending my way with my bottle through the maze of bins toward the front of the room, pretending no hurry, and, when I got there, flipping through the stock he called "new."

The dog looked up. When the door opened I was reaching for a kibble, a blast of cold air wailing; a woman in a fur coat dragged into the store two suitcases, green. She took up what room remained up front and then some; she was almost as wide, front to back if not side to side, as she was tall; she was tall. A hat with a brim like a Frisbee and one central, veiled, chute across its crown, feathers gleaming from the wet snow; beneath it, her mouth pursed like a sea anemone in brine. The first white woman at Record Palace I'd seen, besides me. First woman.

Acie, approaching in the aisle, scowled.

"Acie Stevenson, this place has gone downhill from sea bottom." The woman saw me then, stopped, kept her gaze fastened just above my head, the gaze shiny, steely, not two feet from mine, under a high forehead.

When I smiled she stared until my coat went on.

Outside, the snow was dry and light.

Studs leaned on the console and said a few words to his engineer. A voice returned: "Mike's fritzy. Closer." In the booth, the engineer's face was placid. "Thirty seconds."

"Hello, Studs here. That was William Stevenson, the late William Stevenson. One of bebop's best session bassists died Friday in New York, and we'll be playing his selections during the breaks today. William Stevenson grew up on the South Side of Chicago. He was the son of the only black bank president in the city before 1950, and he got his start with Erskine Tate's band, moved on to Fletcher Henderson's, ended up playin' with Duke Ellington, the great Coleman Hawkins, and Mr. Lester Young, even before he moved to New York City and made thirty-seven records as sideman for the best musicians of the past thirty years. 'Studs,' William Stevenson once said to me, 'being on top only works if you're light on your feet.' Another great of the era has passed prematurely; may he rest in peace."

The engineer turned the dials on his machines and then looked up through the glass. "Fine, Studs. Thanks."

Acie

I know that the Philly tornado is due in and I want this one out of the front. These legal papers put a damper on me. I think it will be easy to get her in back, then I am not so sure. If you ask me this one is pulled tight as any woman I know and they all tight. But I never discount a girl with working parts and besides I want to see what she does. I am not thinking it will lead to nothing but her out of sight.

"Here, I want to show you something," I say.

She looks up bright as if Sonny Rollins him self came in. Whacked chippy.

When I reach for her hand I can tell she is thinking twice. But she takes it and I lead her past the bins toward the quarters I like to call the *estate*. She stops just inside it so I let go her hand and stop too, in kissing space.

"This is my cubby," I say and she is impressed. The chicklets all been hippies once, they like to see their flags upside-down, and she takes it in with my tribute to the Charlie Angels, my kitchen things, my whole setup.

"Nice," she says. Then I know she is not buying, she looks at me with kindness and I know in a lightning strike I am not her bag. So I let her make her exit to the front and think from my wound but mostly from the impending Miss Philly. The girl is a comfortable woman now, leans over to have a say with Dog Ma under my chair, and the door opens. Before I can even get up front to cover the legal papers the empress herself is batting down the hatches for the siege.

"Acie Stevenson. This place is filthy as a pond bottom." It takes a full minute for the girl to give up to Miss Philly.

The girl gives me the eye on her way out. Soon as she is gone, Philly takes no time in starting up. Recording is over and I cue some Nistico. A good session for Roy, his drums ride the top of the tenor like bubbles ride waves.

"Where do you expect me to sleep, Acie?"

"You are the intruder," I say. "No one was issuing invitations."

"Don't I have a right to visit my in-laws?" And then: "Wouldn't be an issue, Acie, if you had not sold your mother's house."

She takes a look at the window grate. I need this charged-up Miss Ann like I need a noose. She slips out of her mink coat with full dramatics but then when she does not find a place suitable to park it, puts it back over her shoulders in a drape. She won't go near the dog and Ma is backed up behind me, watching at her through my legs.

Boss of Bowtie has been after me for some years to in his golden tongue "live a little." "You could use some airing" is what he is after me about, thinking I will expire from a regular routine, but I tell him bills and the urine reserves are all I need to keep me in survival suspense.

Certain shoes have been pacing the sidewalk on the other side all day except now and then they go on a break which they seem to be on at this particular interval. I have been keeping the pistol with me. I got the door ready to wire for the night and Wyans has been doing my running for me. Day before I had a life designed for leisure and now I am in the Hardy Boys.

I do not tell Philly this. I do not know what business brings Bowtie bad drivers but neither he nor Miss Philly will be implicating my crib.

She snorts. "It's bad enough to lose a husband, but then to have the home you shared robbed like a jeweler's—"

"You did not tell me what got took."

"You're his brother. You are the one to fix the losses."

"This your full-moon time?" I ask her and she gives me a look to fry.

"Nothing gets through to that knot of yours." Miss Philly shakes her head and snorts again. "Laziness your name is Acie."

The shoes are back. And as they go by the front door I see the legs, too, and then the legs light out for the other side of the street. Luck has it there is no parked car and in between the passing traffic I see the man himself. He is standing full-spread on the sidewalk opposing and he is regarding me. Cadaver-like.

"So, woman—"

"Don't be womaning me."

"So, woman, what is it you expect me to do." She does not move. "You have had nothing but bullshit and none of this I asked for. So tell it to me." She still is still. "I am waiting."

Philly is a big-bone gal and she walks with a lope. Now she walks the yard to the other end of the front and there is not enough room side to side for the lope. Caged. She squints at me from six feet away now and I wait on her speech. I can wait on it clear to summer.

Miss Philly wants a steak dinner. I tell her I will give her the money and she can go, but she says "What good is that, Acie? You acting nervous to leave your place and me being a woman." Both unfortunate. Both true.

So I am on the horn getting Ming Choy to walk across the street with the noodles and she is in the back clucking. I unlock and pay, and by the time I get the food back to her, Miss Philly is standing with her purse over her arm just waiting. I let the lock stay open for paying customers. The laser-light trigger alarm is on and I got the curtain wide.

I have an affinity for drummers. They are inclined to be easy men. Early '60s Terrence the Trixie absconded me to Phil Black's Ball uptown New York City, where the backdrop band had itself five drummers to every one piano. But I like to hear the crisp sound, the individual. So I tune in now to Roy and his starbursts, but Ronnie Mathews is not bad on the keys here, also, his fingering a breeze.

"What am I going to sit on?" She is one demanding piece of equipment. "If I had known you live like this I would have stayed in New

York." I can tell she is taxing herself working it all out in her thinking. "I can't be staying here, I am not sleeping on that fleabag on the floor."

"What got itself burglarized Philly."

Still standing she picks a sparerib out of the bag and sniffs at it. "Where's the greens?" She hunts open a couple of the white cardboards before she gives up on finding collards. "This and that."

Evasion she is practicing like it is in neon across her. "What," I say, "you and Willy were enterprising somehow? You brought on the burglarizing yourself?"

I see the snow begin a drive against the back windows, over Philly's shoulder. I take enough pills every morning to keep a elephant up. And I do not know about William and what their business implicated. Philly goes at her second rib and she shrugs.

"He has, he had been seeing a whore."

So this is why she is coy. William was always pretty and it was the topic when he took up with Philly.

"Takes money to see a whore and money to buy off the home-sitter."

"He said he did not know she was a whore until he owed her."

"That still does not tell me how he bought *you* off."

This steams her. "He did not have money, Acie Stevenson, and if you think he did, all you have to do is read the papers you got out there. All he did with the Europe-trip money was to pay up the back bills." So she has taken stock of the papers.

The fixings are laid out on the sink shelf and I finish my noodles and foray on to an egg roll when I hear the door clang out front, and when I look I see it is a long-time customer name of Joe. Far as I know he is not a booster but he is wanting something all the time, so I heft back out front, catch the laser alarm. He knocks his hat against his thigh by the White Sox brim and the snowpuffs get the front floor wet.

"Will you watch the merchandise, Joe?"

He is an obsequious cat and he brings it out in me.

Repentant, also. "Sorry, Acie. It's bad out." He takes off a nice pair of driving paws. "I need what you got by the Messengers."

"Is a lot. What year you after?" Art Blakey's Jazz Messengers is a schooling band, and there have been more configurations than I can count.

"Anything."

"Yeah, but is there a cut you are looking for Joe." Joe is suburban raised and now he is playing catch up. He is learning but he is slow.

"The black national anthem? That."

"'Lift up,'" I say. "Hold on." I hear Miss Philly in the back scraping a fork against cardboard, and I want some of the fixings to be left when I get back to her. There are at least six versions of Artie doing "Lift up" and it will take me awhile.

Joe bides his time in the front bins. When I look up from the stock he is studying the back of the glue jacket on an Archie Shepp.

"Leroy Jenkins good?" he asks.

Jenkins does the violin. "Leroy had himself a gift but he sold it out to the squawkers." I get the Messengers in hand. "These are what I got." I lay out in front of him across the bins the LPs with the cuts. "And here are two the management also recommends." I have added a new *Night in Tunisia* and the 1954 date at Birdland. I give him the z and he counts out the cash and while he is counting the door opens again. It's the one stop, Freddy, the LP wholesaler Bowtie is in with. Freddy smiles a wide smile. He is not fazed by the snow water off of his hat and he waits for Joe to finish off and make his exit.

"Little snow, Acie." He is a drink of water and his voice is bass, way bass. I can tell I am nervous about Philly in the back and being nervous about Philly pisses me off. There is no seeing shoes or anything else through the snow at the window.

"Little."

"Just a visit, Acie, to see if you need anything. *And* if you'll be putting something on that account I am carrying for you." He says it up beat. "Only asking, Acie." He tugs an RCA logo out his briefcase. "Brought you a slick." Freddy puts the case down and unbuttons his coat. He usually stays awhile, and any other day he is company. "You catch Jodie with Jackie McLean few weeks back?"

The slick was the alto Jackie's. I take it but I do not engage. "Closing early, Fearless." Fearless Fred goes up against the Verve monolith, and their distribution is high-flying. Warner Elektra and any of the other labels the one stop handles do not match Verve in perks to the owners.

"Oh yeah?" He looks up from his machinations in his case like he is surprised. "Now?" I nod, he shrugs. "I'll be back in a couple days, Acie," easing his coat to again, "you seen Magic last night?" Larry Bird and Magic Johnson, better first-year hoop players I have not seen and last night they were on. I think of the battening down. I say no and Freddy nods as he opens the door.

I still do not lock it for the paying chance, but I put the laser alarm extraordinaire back on.

{

"So this is your reasoning, Philly: the pimp comes to collect." She has made good work of my noodles, too, by the time I get back to her. "William takes up with a girl for a while not knowing her whoredom so her employer sacks a flea-filled crib?"

The woman is truculent. I could be hanging her from the Water Tower.

"That's right," she says, and does her best to look at me straight.

The door bangs again. Nothing like a bad snow to bring out the citizens of Chicago late on a Friday. But when I look, it is Bowtie out of the Jazz Fair, shaking the snow and ready to head his way back to my cubby. I blink the laser so as not to trip the alarm but he does not notice.

"Hakim" (he means Fearless Freddy) "said you were closing early."

I am still stewed for his last night's performance.

He gets near the back and I start to move aside and say to him, "I am needing your assistance." When Bowtie is through the curtain he stares at Miss Philly, nervous. "Your aunt came in, say hello." He still is stopped. "She does not bite."

I get a mumble out of him.

"Philomena here needs a walk upstairs."

"I am *not* staying in some hotel short stop," she says. Her right foot comes down, and Bowtie looks from her to me.

"She is having a problem with the cleanliness quotient in the crib," I say by way of explanation to her nephew.

"I told you the *truth,* Acie Stevenson."

"The Carlton Arms is a fine establishment and they have chairs in their rooms."

She gives Bowtie a commanding regard but he is too edgy to pick up on it. He looks from me to her.

I am sick of the woman already like I am sick of the boy. The snow has slowed and I move out front where outside of the front window no one is passing. Feet outside could be for someone at the Arms, too, I am thinking. Random coincidence. Makes more sense than what I come up with.

Later when I lock and laser up for the evening I find the package of her "valuables" she has got wrapped up with tape beside the throne. They are nothing but my mother's faluting paintings which Philly's ransackers must have overlooked in their intelligence and which she now has carried to safety. With her gone upstairs at the Carlton I can say "stupid woman" and I do.

Wonder of wonders, Bowtie says he will stay the night, must have the fear in him after all, so the magnet for trouble retrieves himself the pallet and goes through the bedcoverings in my setup. The feet seem to be gone for a long time and the snow makes the cars that pass muffle and the cars that are in the corner lot gun. The Jazz Fair is winding up next night, and Bowtie is Boss-of-Bowtie's right-hand man. To think of it gives me a hoot.

He can see under the awning where a knot of spiders has webbed old kill, the shells of insects like slubs in the filament weave, and beyond this, the window opaque and rippled with rain spots. He pushes the doorbell again. Between the house and the rubbled lot next door, a bird lands on the gravel tracks and pecks, furiously, at a patch of weeds beside a Chrysler. Heavy: the toolbox, and he shifts it to the other hand, turns.

"Yup!" A sudden seal-breaking of the door behind him, a whoosh, and an old-timer's voice. An hour's break evaporates like gasoline.

"Furnace cleaning." He lifts the ID strung around his neck on aluminum beads.

From behind his screen the white man leans closer to the card and looks from it to Warren's face. "You're late." No motion to open the door.

The bird has moved on to a clump of plastic flowers in the bed beside the cement step, and now it looks at Warren, too.

Finally the old man stirs. "Well all right. You're a big critter." Warren hears the screen door unlatch and he pushes the button on the door handle, pulls. The man's Skivvies loom into view.

Bowtie

I wanted to be my uncle William, but my grandmother discouraged this. Her house smelled like linseed oil and Tabú, and those smells you could say made me. Art and so forth. Parked on the landing of her circular staircase to play while my grandmother worked, I smelled what wafted from the studio, saw her pass in front of the studio door with a brush in her hand, heard the muted tinkling of a brush being swooshed in a jar of turpentine. That's why I have a nose for talent.

When I was four she slapped me for bringing home a sponge from the house two doors down. "Sponges are for white people." I felt the sting on my cheek. "Remember that." She wore her hair long and straightened and she was light, lighter than my father, lighter than my grandfather, who said to her, "Don't talk like that, Olivia," and, to me, "Don't you ever think that way." In my opinion, my grandfather was overly hopeful.

He brought me a set of plastic green soldiers from the bank and then it was her going on at him about it in his bedroom. He was a devotee of Marcus Garvey. "Your father was con*ceived* during the 1919 disturbance," my grandfather said. "You *will* not forget it," and he made certain I didn't. He liked to listen to the Dizzy tune "Oop-Pop-A-Dop" and to sing along. On Saturdays he took me to Harold's Chicken Shack. I waited under the grated window, listening to the rush of voices and pans banging and music from the kitchen side, for the gizzards in their hot bag. You could say I got my ear from listening to the kitchen pots and the yelling at Harold's.

That's where I fine-tuned my aesthetic. It's based on synesthesia, the fusion of the senses, which is what Harold's was all about. My aesthetic uses what you can see with your eyes and what you can hear with your ears, and the taste of the burnt flecks on the gizzards meeting your tongue.

{

I have been out with some beautiful women, beautiful women. Women with an inner beauty, if you know what I mean, making their breasts or their bellies or their long, shining hair even more of a turn-on, and smart women, women you don't need to tell anything to twice, women who with one remark can make a man stop from making himself a fool. But I still haven't known one as beautiful or as smart as Ivie.

Ivie was my grandmother's studio assistant, and when the brushes made the bell sound in the studio it was she who was cleaning them. When the door was closed, I knew she was modeling, and at a certain point I spent hours coming up with excuses to fall into that room— only time I did, Olivia hit my butt with a stool. Midday Ivie checked the mail in the front hall; she brought the letters to my grandmother in the studio from the famous artist when they came. She had small feet that whisked her to the apartment behind the kitchen and to making herself up for her nights out; on these, she might as well have been a goddess. Those tiny feet in those high, high heels.

Some of her nights out were nights in, when I watched from the stairs glittering gowns enter the foyer, the nights when my grandmother hired in help to pass food on trays.

One day my dad was back. He walked into the house and rolled his eyes at me, but I knew who he was. "You had your self enough of the high life?" I was six but I knew what was what, and what he meant. I'd been to school. Children called me "seddity" but they were jealous of my aesthetic refinement and my life in that house.

My father worshipped his mother in spite of everything he said and did. From the day we left her house I missed her.

"Do not, do *not* squander God's gifts," my grandfather said.

Then came the bouncing years, from Dad's to on the road with my mother, and back to the South Side house and the linseed smell. On the landing I read *Horatio Hornblower* and Booker T. Washington and waited for the studio door to open and Ivie to emerge.

"That is no life for a boy!" My grandmother meant the time I spent with my mother. I sat on the vinyl kitchen chair, swinging my feet over the linoleum, the Payday wrapper on the table in front of me, listening to my father's low reply. "A woman has a right to the company of her offspring no matter the vermin she may be."

With my mother, everything was fast. She would come to my father's house wherever it was at the time and yank me from the door frame and next thing I knew I'd be in her dressing room learning a card trick from a bartender on break, and then off in a car with a backseat the size of Cleveland. "Credit your class," she said. "Take your feet off of the leather interior." But she recognized the genius I was.

My father went to parent-teacher conferences, and after every conference came two days during which my teacher treated me tenderly. Acie lit into me, day and night, about my homework, about my friends, about my attitude, and all I wanted was the peace of my grandmother's house and thought of her as my ally not as the fierce partisan of ordinary potential my father was proving himself to be.

Even I knew my father was a disappointment to my grandmother, but what I knew and he didn't was that my uncle William was a disappointment to her, too.

But then I got high and stayed high. You can learn a lot from mind-altering substances, and they were a large part of what I am today.

"Is this the way I taught you?" My mother, like a pox, on me.

"Well, yes."

My father, miraculously, let up.

Bass, trumpet, piano were not my fortes. I had better ears for the music than fingers. "Just needs an attitude adjustment," my father said. He had lost his sixth place in two years, and we were in temporary quarters again at my grandmother's. I pulled feathers from striped ticking on a pillow, waiting for him to leave so I could roll a joint. "Somewhere you got some gifts to find."

I knew my appreciation was my gift. I had the gift of discernment. But try telling that to my dad.

"You are going to bypass the college over my embalmed body," he said. "My nest egg is not going for your high."

{

My father has wedged himself into an orange chair and is reading a magazine. Sometimes when I come upon him in a neutral place, a public place, he looks so startling I am alarmed I know him, and now he's seeing me and rising. If he'd let me I'd take his arm, even in public, even here.

The room overlooks the pencil building and Wacker Drive, the river and the sweep of downtown; it is an SOM-ian box of a room, its wall of windows lined in steel casement. Forty-two men and three women, facing the table at the interior wall, the speaker and his projected images, see Helmut, caped, enter through the door to their right; forty-one men swivel to watch as he, and three who follow, whisk to the windows and perch, squatting, on the casements. The speaker continues, the graphs and elevations dry and his talk impassioned. The image of a building, a panopticon in a prairie, at last clicks onto the screen. He calls for questions.

"Yes!" Helmut calls from the back of the room, and continues in his thick accent. "It is a construction of genius, a sculpture, a paean to form. Why do you believe you need to justify it with data? Throw the tables away!"

Cindy

Sleet striped the windows of the dorm on Thanksgiving. Down Blackstone, out my dorm window, the glimmering neon of Valois: See Your Food cafeteria and, on the corner, the Hotel Savoy, where that morning a tuxedoed waiter had brought me two eggs over easy, domed, on a tablecloth, for $2.65.

Otto Mueller, Emil Nolde, Ernst Ludwig Kirschner, Oskar Kokoschka—if the color plates of the *Blaue Reiter* or *Die Brücke,* or of any of the German Expressionists, fuzzed before your eyes, they became kaleidoscopic. I experimented with this, then out the window, then back to the book. Such saturated hues. What did Acie do on Thanksgiving? Harnett was booked.

Focus. I tried. Tried on this: *In Beckmann's painting,* Circus Caravan, *painted as it was in 1949, the ringmaster attends a version of Manet's reclining Olympia as though he is her sentinel. By 1940, Beckmann's iconography has deepened its cryptic symbolism and, after several years of residence in Amsterdam, having fled Berlin and Nazi fervor, he has returned to the more attenuated Gothic style of his youth.*

Dogmeat and still nine hundred words to go.

Cars turning in off Lake Shore Drive near the Museum of Science and Industry, at the edge of the window, streaming in the wet gray along the boulevard where university met ghetto, the *DMZ*. Would it be worse to call Mom or to not? The tumble of note clusters in Muhal Richard Abrams's solo piano on "D Song" dipping to the bottom of the keyboard, getting stuck, rising, then the sharp staccato of licking the high C-sharp pierced, until Abrams descended the scales. Something like rain, offbeat and irregular, in the notes' runs on the vinyl disc.

Rather read than write. Did Archie Shepp, did Charles Mingus or Jeanne Lee, would they rather listen than play? Maybe Jeanne. The woman.

Listening, imagining Abrams standing at the keyboard, holding the strings in the grand piano firm with one hand, then strumming them with the other to get a mute, muffled whirr. Releasing them, the strum a glissando. Several thuds reverberated the whole of the machine's notes, and gongs began.

Or knocking. But it was someone at the door. I turned the Abrams down, smoothed out the bed, closed off the bathroom. Harnett?

"Yes?" Turning the knob, springing the door. A woman with orange hair in a bowl-cut stood in the hall.

"Sorry to bother you," she said, "but my toilet's fucked and they can't get a plumber on Thanksgiving they're telling me, and I really need to take a shit." No chance to react, she was pushing past me and into the bathroom. "There's hardly anybody on the floor," the woman said from behind the bathroom door, "just a couple of Orientals."

I couldn't think what to say. Finally, "Where is your room?" I as alert to a scam as the next.

"Next door!" Her muffled voice surprised. "Oh—I just dyed my hair. For the holiday."

I couldn't recall or visualize any of my neighbors, suddenly. No wonder I was a lousy art historian. *So* observant!—but that was my mother's voice.

The toilet flushed. Water ran. Imagining my neighbor drying off on my towel. "Thanks—Happy Thanksgiving!" She took me in for a moment, a foot out the door and a foot in. Then she swung the door out slamming it between us, and all that was left was the smell of her shit.

My father, nights before he left for good. His clarinet case behind him on the kitchen table, he standing at the sink, the tub of my mother's chicken open beside him on the counter and his fingers long and girl-like, greasy with the skin, pulling the threads of chicken to his mouth. Then, suddenly, coughing. A spluttering cough, spiky, insistent. In the living room, beyond the kitchen island, I bent toward the television and turned the volume knob up. Coughing like on the choking posters.

Long, indolent seconds. My hands at my ears. Counting the cigarettes stubbed in the ashtray by the couch.

The coughing stopped. He ran water in the sink, opened the refrigerator door, I heard him fart. Rounding the island toward the door between us, his clarinet box like a gun case from T.H.R.U.S.H.

"Little bitch." Glaring at me. "Little bitch."

"Miss Cindy."

Wondering if sleeping with Harnett again the night before showed. The air in the shop, electric with bebop. Unison trumpet, alto, tenor, then the tenor spun off, one by one horns taking sixteen bars each, cymbal-glistening and hi-hat clapping, a propulsive snare, bright piano.

Acie on the volume dial.

"The dragon exists to make the hero, Albert Murray wrote that. You know he also wrote that *avant-garde* is military for the advance troop, so it is only a natural fact that by the time the rest of the troops reach the battleground the originals are lying on the stretchers. You go to school. You ever read Albert Murray?"

I shook my head. Harnett's smell was still on me.

"What sign are you, we were asking." Acie's right eye wandering toward Pluto and me half tuned in.

"Sagittarius."

"Sagittarius? As in the half beast?" I smiled, expansive today for me, ready to humor Mom. "No wonder you are a slippery chick—or Mizzz. When is it?"

"What?"

"Your birthday." He: expansive, too. Really expansive.

"Couple days." My hopes of ignoring the birthday had been dashed that morning by a package from my uncle, baby blue nylon nightie.

Acie stared into space for a while and then he said, "*Days.* You will be needing recog*n*ition." Not just expansive: jacked. Rifling through the play copies of LPs piled beside him, most without covers. In paper sleeves.

The unison brass had taken over again, crested a bridge, coasted to a corny wrap-up.

This was one way to come up with a postcoital gift. The curve beneath Harnett's shoulder swung before my eyes, away again.

And then there was a motion on my right. A stooped older man in a car coat looking at the bins in the back, bins late in the alphabet—Randy Weston, maybe, or Ben Webster, Dicky Wells. The man raised his head, lowered it like a duck, muttered something I didn't catch .

"Girl. You celebrate." Acie holding out a stack, I pretending awe at its size. Two copies of the same disco mix by Smokey Robinson, an old Grant Green, an Arthur Blythe I'd bought from him: all stamped PROMOTION COPY/NOT FOR SALE. He added an LP by Enrico Rava to the pile. "For those movie moments," he said.

"How about you come back at 6 and I take you to Joel's duel to-night for your birthday." One of Jazz Lounge's extravaganzas at the Blackstone Hotel, Long Tall Dexter versus Little Johnny Griffin, post-ers rainbow-bled like the fight notices along Chicago streets, a one-night engagement. I'd wanted to go.

But Acie, on the town? Today, his odd garrulity. I knew I could just leave, study, leave Acie and his weirdness to Acie and his weirdness. Acie was not my life.

"Your dog die?"

"I don't have a dog," I said, and then before I could stop myself, "6?"

Acie nodding, affecting a disinterested look. I wasn't fooled.

Outside, a determined sun on snowbanks; a passing truck sound-ing like a brook down the middle of Clark Street, the truck slopping through the slush, turning onto Chicago Avenue. I had a stack of re-cords, no bag, and five hours to kill on the edge of the Gold Coast. For this, God had invented bars.

All the jukebox seemed to play was "Fly Me to the Moon," but I was too lazy to go over there and check it out myself; a uniformed fellow, Knickerbocker lobby man, kept ducking around the door and programming it again. Woman bartender, a sparkle off the mirrored bottles, a coaster quilted with JOHNNY WALKER BLACK—THE CONNOISSEUR BLEND, no lame losers, no wind, joy. I chased the amber with a dark brew and then took it to the head.

Three figures stand in front of Record Palace *looking up. A lumpy and large man—in orange slacks and flip-flops, his hair Jehri-Curled into locks, one eye off—squints as though he has emerged from hibernation, a little shook by the light. A trim man in a black sports jacket and a kufi wipes his mouth solidly with his cupped palm and bends his head back again, surveying the sky. A woman in a fur coat holds onto her hat to keep it from exposing her thinning hair, scraped back across her scalp like a man's. They stand clear of the melting snowbank with their hands at their heads—sailors at salute, a mirage.*

Acie

In the morning there is even sun through the back window. The vehicles progressing on State Street slop and the thaw is on. No shoes to be seen, Philly in the hotel, my dick continent, I think there may be a new day dawning. Bowtie comes out of the back looking slept. He has a cup of coffee for me in his grip, and another stewing on the stove. Old Mills Brothers on the platter-turner. This is the way a man's life should be I think. Way mine has been until now.

Bowtie says Johnson at the Carlton Arms would not take my money for Philly, and he pulls it out of his trousers and hands it over to me and then he goes back for his coffee. Bowtie has begged me for the cash off and on but he will not just take it which I know comes out of my genetic constitution. All this bodes so good I feel generous.

"Johnson I owe you," I say in the phone. Johnson grunts in his end. "And will you tell that woman I am taking her to breakfast? I will be sending the son around for her." Johnson growls and I hear the dial tone. I let Bowtie nurse his coffee and I look at his shirtless chest and the scar across his collarbone and think once I had that chest and better.

"Don't wear the flip-flops, Acie," Bowtie says.

Embarrassing the heir is another promising endeavor. "Warm as a woman," I say. "Look at that sun."

My footwear of choice is a perennial beef with him. He gets his nag from the maternal line.

He is not even listening to himself, hardly me. Bowtie is gnawing at his own cheek and staring with a glaze at the dog. I feed Ma kibbles one at a time from the bag and she is pert at attention for them. Philly ate half my order last night and I am hard up for some bacon.

Bowtie shakes himself. "That woman is big."

"Six months in front, nine months behind," I say.

"Ever notice her shoes?" Bowtie tell me. "In New York they're piled up like logs by a fire."

There is a catch at the moment. Bowtie.

"When have you been to her place!"

"I saw her, I saw her and William when I was there in August. I told you."

"And here I am thinking you did not know your uncle enough to be missing him."

"I told you, Acie."

"Like hell."

Could spoil a day, but it will not. I send Bowtie upstairs to collect Philomena in all her slendiferous getup. By the time she comes down in a hat the size of Cleveland, I got the gate double-locked and am parting the slush on the steps with my slap shoes. Bowtie points out an icicle on the roof. We all look up at the melt.

{

Philly did not have a bad night in the Arms and now she seems to think this is a estimable vacation. She thinks maybe she will go to Cabrini Green to look up a sister. And Bowtie with good sleep and sun seems less Nervous Nelly, so I sit them right at breakfast and then once I eat I come back to open the shop. I see him standing out front before I am on the block.

This time like he is waiting for me to open, he does not move.

I watch him straight on as I open the gate without looking, so often have I done it. He is an old man plain to see, even I am a knee-high by him, and he looks at me steady back but does not converse. The sun is on his hat and the shadow of the brim eats his face, still I can tell he is eyeballing me. He follows me into the store and I go to the back wall and adjust the lighting for the appropriate mood. Bright. I got them all up and he stands patient with his sweaty mitts behind his coat waiting.

"What you got by the Cab Jivers?" His voice is a nest of hornets, and I do not like his question. The Cab Jivers was a performing spin-off of Cab Calloway's sidemen and on the only recording they ever made I was at the dials. Only thing I ever produced which may account for why the recording was never printed.

Band the Cab Jivers still has a rep, but no lowlife could be knowing about the studio session. The Iguana still looks at me but I can match a stare-down and I do.

"What would you be looking for." I will play along until he tips his hand.

"1947 date. In New York. You know it?" The rasp in his voice is like the death rattle itself, and the dog Ma gets up a low growl.

"No." I stare harder with the tilt-up so he gets the full effect of my straying eye. "What was in the book?"

"Do you have *any*thing by the Cab, Brotherman?" I dislike this particular expression, but I do not indicate my displeasure. Nor do I indicate my displeasure at the man's entire perspicacity. I gesture at the bins behind and say, "Look to yourself," cool as the experienced player that I am. In the silence except for the clicking noise of the LPs in the bins I mind that he is the trespasser and all I need to do is wait him out. Less I say, the tighter the leash I got him on.

Joe last night looking for Blakey puts me in the mood to hear some. The buzz has been on about the piano player on the new one, I turn it on and up.

The white girl comes in. Feel like Grave Digger Jones here.

Whatever is transpiring is not going to involve me in anything flighty with a white girl. I keep my eye on the man but I carry on with her like nothing is up. She tells me her birthday is around the corner, which is a good excuse to cover my brother's papers from view with a stack of birthday LPs while I keep on my job about the man.

"Chill in the air," the man says when I give her the stack.

"How about you come back at 6 and I take you to Joelly's duel tonight for your birthday." The girl turns even whiter, then she turns orange, then finally she quits the place. I say not to get the headaches from the books.

The man steps back from the bin and lights himself a cigarette. I neglect to bring to his attention the city ordinance on smoking in a business establishment.

"Wonderful day," the Iguana says. "Marvelous day."

I think to point out he got the wrong end of the alphabet for Calloway but the Cs are right behind me and this is not where I need him. "Find what you aiming?" I ask him.

His hand with the cigarette does a wave. "Not important." It is almost a freakish wave which would not make the Iguana less trouble.

Dog Ma still in the low growl.

"Enjoy your breakfast, brotherman?"

I act for a few minutes like this was not said. I bend over Ma with a kibble and when I come up I have this Iguana fixed in my eye.

"If you have business with me, say it."

He drops his lung-buster under his foot and on my floor. He looks up to look out the window and in his voice he says, "You may be finding yourself making a small loan."

"And your business is the hustle."

"Brotherman, this be *your* business. I am telling *you.*"

I still have my eye clamped on him and he has his two still at the window. "Sounds to me like botheration, not information. *Brotherman.*"

The Iguana sees me now but the face is still set up in dark. This one is old. "A loan. Helping a relation in need."

He stirs himself and comes around the bins on my side. It is the smug that tests my cool.

"Shame you don't have the Cab Jivers." I smell him under my nose when he takes the turn past and on to the door. The dog barks. "Hear they caught a Dizzy spitball and took Cab out over the top."

Some sell milk, some sell damages is what I have observed. "No call for it." The Iguana nods and the door bangs behind him.

When his shoes creep themselves off, I am on the horn to my man Wyans who I know is due by. When I say "Cashing in, Wyans," all the man has to say in reply is, "About time." What I know I tell: Bowtie run off the road and this Iguana at me; Cab Jivers recording no one has business knowing, on the tongue of this Iguana; Philly's crib tore up and her gone to Cabrini—"whatever you can turn up, Wyans, is more than what I know."

William Stevenson's brother, I used to get, *how is it being. You must get the girls, your mama must be proud.* Well the mama was proud because she got to say *the arts* and *my son* in the same sentence. However, it did not set me up with the ladies any that I could see. And I got it on with Bowtie's ma due to her believing I was a commercial man with money to make. Question should have been how it is knowing who I know. Like Wyans.

"Sick of waiting on the women today anyhow," Wyans says. So I give the henpecked a hole in the coop. Meanwhile not hide nor hair come in further from Miss Philly nor from Bowtie but I am not their keeper.

When the girl comes back she is one odoriferous chick. My luck to get the lush but I do take the opportunity to partake of a Colt before she gets on my case to wear shoes and lock up. Socks I will do but I am not putting on the leathers for Joelly this time.

I can live for a long time in uncertainty.

The Iguana does not know that this woman with my family name, this Miss Philomena Stevenson on the high hat hog, means nothing. She may be in my hair but she does not reside in my head. And if the *relation* be the offspring, just get to him first and save me the bother.

Dex and Johnny are more show than blow tonight. Before I know it I am wet and I tell the chicklet I will be back. She seems to be enjoying herself and from the smell of her this does not surprise me.

My situation appears to be omnipresent. In the hotel hall the Iguana's snakeskin head talks to a security for the motherland in a royal dashiki along the wall to my left. Peepers of the Iguana on me like lice and I mind them as I pass by.

Not a good sign, the Iguana moving in on my recreation. Ushers are sticky as syrup. I shake them off, I know where I am headed.

In case of surprises I take the corners tight for my size. The brown carpet is redundified with pink roses and the roses go up the wall.

Once I got the zipper down, the dick does not perform. I blot at the trousers with some TP and wait and hear the drip at the urinals and a couple of cats slapping each other five, happy. I hear the door open and a quieting fast, so I think the two happies are gone until a muttering and then a shuffle happens, then the door again and the dashiki passes the stall door into no stall and comes back along the other direction until the red and yellow pattern of the dashiki cloth is sitting outside my stall like he is doing some serious primping in the gaper.

It is a wonder my dick has not fallen off with abuse. The start of this day I do not even remember but I know I was a fool to think I was home free.

North on State Street, and off Rush Street in the pit of the Gold Coast, the heir to the Playboy empire shifts her pillow, rises, slides on slippers, and scuffs down the hall to the room with the round bed. Christie crosses it and goes down the back corridor, through the kitchen, and around the back stairwell. There she hits the lights. Under a green fluorescent glow, bunk bed after bunk bed in the mammoth room stack like headstones in a George Romero pan. The walls, a deep pink, are pocked and streaked.

She stands for a while, shivers, and then makes her way from the other door out to the hall leading through the bowling alley and to the underwater bar. She can remember it in use: a woman swimming up to the window in the wall and mooning a congressman who had softened in the palm of his drink. Kon-Tiki masks stud the bar shelves. The room, dank, seedy, was a kingdom her father had ruled like a class.

Cindy

{

Back of the room was all that remained after Acie's stalling and my getting a taxi, finally. Lit up like Christmas, outfitted for eighteenth-century dances: wedding-cake trim and ceiling, huge brocaded draperies reaching fourteen, fifteen feet high. The stage a platform at one end covered with the hotel's red bedspreads: regal, at a distance. Trucks of folding chairs in long, wavering rows fanning out beyond the stage, the audience dressed for church roaring under bright lights, before the show had even started. Glum in a ruffled dress, a girl kicked the back of a chair. Late we were, but no sign yet of anything beginning.

People nodded to Acie without speaking. A woman in a print pantsuit brought him a folding chair, not looking at me, Acie sitting down on it without his usual cavalier routine. I could tell he was getting the most out of being out with a girl, young, white.

I was alert now, my high cleared, killed by cold, pretzels with the chasers. I, fine. Relieved that it didn't seem to be about *me*, it wasn't a date.

The sidemen adjusting their equipment: straight Chicago hoisters, Wilbur Campbell on drums and Rufus Reid on bass, back from New

York for the date. From an aisle, the city's honorary jazz dad, Von Freeman, tenor and father of tenor Chico, leaning into a row, taking someone's hand, shaking it, straightening, giving a small salute to the row behind.

I looked out over the crowd for Harnett on the off chance he had come, it not being his kind of jazz: the show and blow, the hamming for the audience, swapping fours with the drummer before going back to the head. But it wasn't my dad's either: besides the skin color, this was bebop that *charged*.

"I'm Joel Berger and this is the Jazz Lounge at the Blackstone Hotel; thank you for coming." A rumble rolled over the room and Joel Berger's fallen face smirked above the red bedspreads, adjusting the mike.

Acie, bored by not seeing, his eye fixed on the far wall and his lids half closed. "Before I introduce tonight's contestants, Mr. Long Tall Dexter Gordon" (roar) "and The Little Giant, Mr. Johnny Griffin," (roar) "I want to mention a few of our upcoming appearances." Not a half-note over the Joel Berger's usual disinflection.

And then the band swung into "Strollin'," a Dexter song.

With Johnny Griffin's first solo the crowd began whooping; I, knowing it was not that he was the favorite but that he was given points for picking Long Tall Dexter's song.

"I got to go," Acie said, suddenly rising. "Take the chair so as nobody else gets it while I am gone." Dexter cut in, the stage dissolving behind Acie who held the front of his pants in a fist. Slumping into the chair, missing the view I'd had standing, impatient for Acie's return, I felt the thirst, back now, setting in.

Johnny Griffin was short, but I could see the top of Dexter Gordon's hair, and occasionally his steady face, blowing, as the heads in front of me shifted their alignments. The crowd whistled, shouted. Women popping up here and there as though they were testifying, making a kind of power salute in their finery. Dexter was the traditional ladies' man, Johnny for those who liked men small, feisty, fast.

Me, I was privileged to be with a fat old black man in a hairnet who smelled. Not confusing this with romance.

Where was he? The tenors finished "I Should Care," began "I Told You So."

A crowd at the door to the banquet room. No mass that was Acie, but a kufi in the blue and gold that was Harnett's, turned toward the stage. He came after all. Harnett.

If I left Acie's seat I'd lose it, so I listened, waited. "Autumn Leaves." "The Apartment." "Monk's Dream." "Antabus." On "When We Were One," I moved. Crowd surrounding me like the ballad itself, I keeping the kufi in my sights.

But when I got nearer to the door it wasn't Harnett. I regretted losing Acie's chair: maybe Acie was embarrassed by the wet on his pants, waited for it to dry, or maybe he was taking a walk, would be back in a minute. Standing-room crowd clogging the rear of the room by the door, uncharitable with space, tense, disdainful, hard. A whiff of wooziness. The woman beside me sniffed.

On the red stage Long and Tall Dexter bowed his head as he played. Wilting legato, his articulation clear but soft on the attack. With each song the instrumentalists trading solos, already a long set. I looked back and forth, door behind me, stage, a restless couple behind me glaring back.

"Body and Soul." Tenors milking the battle, driving themselves hard, signalling the last number to the crowd, man in the back row already standing for the ovation, swaying and clapping with the crescendo, bouncers at the far wall splitting their attention between the audience and the stage. Johnny Griffin leapt into a high, showy cascade, while Dexter tried to upstage him with a fully blown melody, low register, catching me in the throat. Magic doing its work, I knew, but I couldn't help soaring anyway. So many years of music, so much of a brawny city, so many lives coming together, pivoting in this beat. I was infected by the montage I'd seen and the stories it had woven, and I felt tears again in my eyes, tears to be here, to be the interloper, by witnessing responsible for what I didn't yet know. *It's all about* you. But that, that voice, my mother's.

Passes at eight different endings. As the musicians thwarted each and took off again, the crowd yelled; by the third round the audience was on its feet. The last note fading in the whoops and the roar, being funneled toward the exit in the surge, still swollen, moved; I looked at my watch. Acie had been gone over an hour: 10:10.

With the surge, outside. Clumps stamping, their breaths and speech icing in the air, couples, families, heading off. No Acie. I fought back through the exit, a bouncer in the foyer, his arms folded over his shirt, watching two white guys leave, each with a bag slung over his shoulder and the zipper down on a military parka.

I didn't expect Acie's behavior to conform to what I knew. The alternatives were many. He'd gotten bored, gone back up to Record Palace. Gone for a pint or a fix—didn't know, did I—drugged in a doorway two blocks away. Maybe sick, alone in the men's room, or sick of me, finding a way of scaring me off. Maybe I should have a drink and sort it out.

"Hi," I said, bald bouncer raising his eyes skyward. "Listen, I think my friend may be sick in the men's room. Would you check for me?"

The crowd in the foyer thin, although some still in the ballroom, lingering in the bright lights, watching the musicians break down the stand.

"Can't leave my spot," he said. "Ask someone else." Two hands on the front of his dashiki, smoothing, then a shift. "What does your friend look like?"

"About six three, three hundred pounds," I said. "Black, long hair."

A change in his expression, now the bouncer volunteering, "I'll look to it," disappearing down the staircase beside the revolving door.

Out the exit doors a few groups straggled, smoking and laughing, their breath white under the canopy lights. Cars whizzed on Roosevelt Boulevard, toward the Dan Ryan Expressway, from Lake Shore Drive. Then a changed light made it still.

Minutes passing, then the bouncer rounding back up the stairs, shaking his head. "Nobody there," going on past me into the ballroom. I could see him through the open door crossing toward the stage where bright shirts were coiling wires. Doughy *Down Beat* critic Herb Johnson following Joel Berger down the aisle, training a small tape recorder ahead of him like a Geiger counter. Shimmering chandelier.

It might have been mild for December to Chicagoans but it was cold to me. What should I do? Go by the store? Couldn't have lost him, more likely that Acie had lost me, intentionally, even. Not belonging with art buffs didn't make me belong with Acie—even with Harnett for that matter. Late, cold, a mug of Irish coffee I imagined, or without the coffee, a shot, any whiskey, to fortify. To prepare.

I'd seen paintings by Whistler that dissolved into blackness except for small episodes of light, pin dots, sometimes washes: the lake beyond the drive on my right, walking north. Chicago Loop shuttered tight and liquorless.

The slush was frozen solid, precarious walking. Gelled ice, on grass blades in the split tar of the State Street car lot, crunching under my boots. The expressway's entrance sparkling in the dark, I pretended this was L.A., the cold an evening's fluke. Ahead lights, dull rumble of Rush Street, here deserted except for passing cars, Lincolns and Audis, women sleek on the passenger seats in the dashboards' glow. It had been a long walk from the South Loop over tundra.

The gate was pulled and locked across the basement front but now I knew to look for a light in the back room. Crouched before the low window, peering through the dirt and the dark. Nothing. He could be asleep. Should I holler?

If it had been me bailing out on someone else, it would piss me off to be followed. But what reason had I given Acie to ditch me? Does he need one? Ditched; I was ditched.

Who can I turn to?

He must be sixty years old, and he has been taking care of himself for a long time.

I thought about the trek back over ice to the Loop for the number one bus to the South Side. Two men bent on a bender came down the sidewalk, I rose from my crouch, nodding, *jump them for their bottles:* a flash. Hooting together, eyeing me, their bags in gloveless hands, they whistled, passed.

I couldn't just stand here.

Harnett had a TV. Two beers in the back of the fridge still. Was it too late?

On Rush Street, couples on dates wove under neon signs, music flushed from doorways. Saturday night. Inside the door to Gino's Place a pay telephone—resisting going in, swizzling a stool, fortifying. Quarter, Harnett's number, long rings. No answer.

A south-bound bus pulled into the Oak Street light and stopped. Cold fingers, cold pocket, enough there for a fare and transfer.

Fewer than five hours later I bolted awake, 4:30, black as ink beyond the dorm. Knowing Acie's phone worked only intermittently, either he turned the ring off so he couldn't hear it or Ma Bell disconnected it for nonpayment, I found the number in the white pages, *Record Palace.* Star of a plane in the window. The phone rang a long time. "Yeah?"

Spooked. The wrong number. "Who is this?"

"Who's asking?" Voice sleepy and irritated. Jesus. It was.

"*Harnett?*"

"Who's this?"

No, I dialed the right one. It's in front of me, phone book spread. "Cindy. It's Cindy. Harnett? What are you doing at Acie's?"

Pause, audible collecting, composing, fumbling, "I'm staying here. How did you know I was here?"

"I didn't." Swam. Slammed. "I'm calling *Acie.*"

Harnett, pushing sleep away, I knew that state of his. Rustling. "Let me see."

"Harnett, what are you doing there? Is *he* there?" Jesus.

"Hold on." A rustle, pause. "I don't know, he's not here. Must not have gotten in." Him shaking more sleep from himself, scrape of the receiver. "How are you, girl?"

Huh? "What are you doing there, Harnett?"

"Stayed here last night." Audible stretching, his voice cracking. "He's my father. Biologically speaking. What time is it?"

Jesus, a father, Acie a father, Harnett his son. "Your *father?*" I had never imagined Acie a father. "I can't believe this. Your *father?*" The two—

"Meant to tell you." Nervousness in his laugh. "You should listen to my show this morning, I'm playing that cut from 'Horn Culture.'"

"I *asked* you about him."

"What time is it?"

"I *asked* you that time."

"What time *is* it?"

"Four-thirty. He didn't come back last night?"

I heard Harnett move around with the phone receiver at his ear, imagined him carrying the phone. Water ran. Still assimilating: Harnett, Acie. "Harnett." I looked out at the DMZ, one lone car slicking its lights on the street.

"Did you see him at the Jazz Lounge show last night? I caught the Hal Ra Ru and I think he went to the Blackstone. Thought you wanted to go to that."

"I did, I went with him but midway through the set he left." Inbreath, Harnett's, through the line. "I asked you if you knew the store, you didn't—"

"What are you saying, 'left'?"

"—say—why? He went to the bathroom and didn't come back."

"Oh shit. Shit."

"What?"

"Nothing."

"You stay there," I said. "I'll come to the Palace."

"No need, girl. Stay—" But the phone was halfway to the cradle.

One bagged beer for the journey, guard asleep in the lobby, iced air. Dressed for 5 a.m. deep in a Chicago December.

A year before, I had sat in the Fairlane in the garage lot off 405 with the windows rolled up, knowing I couldn't replace the blown retread, or the axle or the transmission I'd just been warned would kill me soon. Cases of liquor in the back bed for my mother. "I'm not going to bail that heap out—you bought it, you fix it. You can't run to me like a baby." Cars rushing past on the strip.

More than anything else it had been lack of a car that meant I'd go to the University of Chicago and not to St. Louis, where I would have needed one, and where paintings by Beckmann were abundant. Bobbi had said, "You don't need a car in Chicago." And: "Get yourself some *down*." Then I was on my own.

On the IC platform, the wind cut like a scalpel. A commuter in green scrubs knocked a clot of ice with his shoe in the pool of light beneath the overhang; blowing snowflakes shone against the dark surround. In Harnett's quaver I'd heard the instinct to dissemble, and the dread of this cut, too. Harnett just happened to fall in with me, *sure*. Girl

without ties, mooning around his dad—a music fan, easy to seduce.
But why?

On the horizon, beyond the lake, a strip of shadowy light glinted.
By 6:30, by the time I'd make it there, the sun would be almost up.

"Mrs. Mayor." Behind Jesse, at the door to the Herronner's office, are fourteen or fifteen men in suits and half a dozen cameras. A flash discharges. "I am at your disposal. If you are in need of strike negotiation, just as I have demonstrated on the national and on the international level, I will make myself and my gifts of mediation available to the health of this city. Let it never be said that one building burned to the ground in Chicago, or that one Chicago child lost her life to fire because disagreements with the present administration over the levels of affirmative-action hiring precluded this citizen from serving his city in a time of trials."

Everyone present knows a settlement has already been reached.

Acie

"If that don't take the cake."

This is what I hear when I wake up. I am inside a comedy heaven. I am inside the cartoons seeing stars. Another voice, high as in tenor and high as in high, follows the first one. ". . . God in 1929 outside of a little hotel in Baltimore . . . and I heard a voice call out to me down . . ." This voice tears him self up and I got the shakes. He laughs like a hyena in heat.

I have felt like the end for some years but this is worse. And I get to feel like this in a cage with a Pryor budhead.

I hear a door creak to and "Excuse me," and I smell that verminous Pine-Sol smell. I try to feel my can and I am working on opening the eye. Over the hyena voice comes a bang. "Anybody in here?"

It is a peckerwood and I am in a shithole he has come to clean. My can is locked into a space between the throne and the side wall to fit a toothpick. I move the neck but it seems to have a direct line to the teeth. Money. Keys. Nuts. My special charm. All accounted for.

"Anybody in here?"

"Ub" appears to be the sound I am equipped to make.

"You okay in there?"

Cracker. "Get out of my face and I will flush."

I see where there is blood. I test the body parts. My royal nose, intact. Even the knees as I extract my can from its perch are working but this brings on pain that shoots into the back and up the arm so I get the tear-eyes just moving the can to the throne. I cannot tell what it is that has my head so sore. I reach for my net and in the hand I bring back is the hair I once got in the blood now I do not.

Three men are in the room with me when I make for the mirror. Two of them are in fine form and they stop their noise making and gape. One is the innocent and he puts his head down to his bucket fast. In the glass is a fright with a mohawk.

The hyena voice says, "You should be getting a white coat on that."

I am seeing the blood. Why in everloving, I think. Why in everloving? If that woman has come into town to fill my life with trouble like she filled William's—

"Do you want an ambulance?" The cleaning man does not look up from the bucket, even talking. "I'll call one for you." Lots of this blood. "You okay?"

Sink is full of other people's crunt. I turn on the water. "I could use your hat," I say, turning to the cat with the hyena. Knit cap will stretch on this mess.

"Hey, Pops," and he backs himself up some, "you should not be putting no hat of somebody's on that head as it is."

I feel the water for its temperature and look for the soap. "Why, you got the bugs?"

"Not me, no," he says, then, "here," and he hands it over. Rubbing appears to have left me no skin behind the ears and I have never known pain until the hat goes on. I look dangerous. Soon as they hand over the hat the brothers hightail it. The cracker goes with them to call his ambulance but he will not be disappointed to find me gone.

I have a mind to kill Bowtie for them. I would think he would be easier to follow than his paternal benefactor. Know-nothing, my hat.

Philly is the likelier progenitor of my persecution. I am beginning to think she concocted the heart give-out story and that William was running with some wild cats is more like it.

It is barely light, and there is a mean hawk blowing off the lake that tears into my scalp through the knitting in the cap. Traffic is quiet in this part of downtown early on a Sunday. Pawn-shop gate next door is half cracked, but I am in no way to shop. A taxi wheels itself in and out; then another; finally I pull my collar over the scrapes on my neck and one doesn't see well enough until it is too late for him.

"State and Chicago," I say. I got my money still.

At Ohio I see what looks to be the girl walking. Only 6 a.m. not much light and she wrapped up and going my way. Now I know what she looks like—stringy white rendition of Maxine Sullivan in the early days, skinny, only with that scabby straw hair. Actually does not look like her at all. Like the time Nelson was trying to explain what Benny Goodman looks like to a bozo and it come out: *You know the Duke? Take out all the color and a foot off the top and add ten pounds and glasses and you got yourself Goodman.* The hard way home is a good selection for the fun loving.

"Pull over." The driver looks at me and he does not de-accelerate a mite. "I said pull over." He is a puffy white driver but I cut a more imposing figure. He complies now and I pull the hat down on the raw skin so as a pain tears from the scalp to the brain.

I do not blame the girl getting high hatted. She will not look at this taxi until I say "Miss Cindy!" Then she spins like Cassius Clay. She has got a look of the anticipation on her.

"Acie?"

Barely 7 in the morning. She is a sight.

The chippy opens the door on the other side of the vehicle and next thing I know she is next to me. "Jesus, what happened?"

"You saved me just in the nick of time, princess. Give me some sugar." I indicate my cheek next to my lips but the girl ignores that. She is smarter than a man would expect on looking.

Supreme exhaustion falls upon me. I can tell she wants to take off the hat and look at the damages but that she does not want to touch me. Chicklets.

"What happened?"

I will just rest my head at this light before mine. "I got myself a new configuration, do you like it? Hope you got your self lucky after the music last night."

"Stop joking." Her face is still set up like cement.

It is brighter out of the window but not by much, which means snow. The lazy flakes are happening now but the overcast makes this just the startup. I need my self a rest.

Lights on in the shop but there has been no B & E as the gate is unimpaired. Philly does not have the key so my money is on Bowtie. If Bowtie has deigned to drop by I am extracting his teeth.

"Harnett!" the girl is yelling, with me leaning on her hard enough to feel a fine can.

"You know Bowtie?" I say. The stringy girl knows the offspring. "What Am I Waiting For" by the O'Jays is blaring on *my* turntable.

"What?" She does not hear for her rattling the gate. Bowtie's hangdog snout appears and his saucer eyes.

"Shit, Acie," he says, unlocking. "Shit."

I am feeling like the white sheriff on *Gunsmoke* with Miss Kitty. The girl has at me with a wetted-down T-shirt and even in pain there is a particular gratification in being attended by a girl who is not getting paid to nurse. Bowtie is sitting opposite looking at me over the steam from his coffee and looking then at the floor with *Shit* issuing out his mouth. He *acts* pitiful but the music he has on, some of the harmmelodic shit, designed to prove he is the young and unscathed one and I am the one prone to a headache.

First thing he did was put on his kufi when we came in and it is down at his eyebrows. Over the years other people have said Bowtie talks but I have not seen it. His ma folds the ears so he may not have to.

"If you know why I am now embroiled in your enterprising, it is your time to say," I start in with him. I keep the peep on him, too, to see how forward he may be with the girl. Fact of her coming in all this time and not mentioning her being one with the Bow does not endear her stanky self. She daubs me slow so as not to raise the blood again, but it is not what you would call a bedside manner that she has with me or my head.

·"I have to go do my show and I've got to work today. Then I'll come back." Son of ages, my son.

"Do not be bringing your magnetized self back around here," I say. "The man do not care, he is interested in *you*." I could have a considerable effect on someone, even a relation, but the drippy droopy bass-and-tenor show on the hi-fi is getting the best of me. "Why is it we have to listen to this shit."

Bowtie has always thought himself too smart to be instructed. "I've got the show, I've got to be at the Bebop Shop by 2. I'll talk with you later. Got to get the el."

"You got transportation."

He looks away and then down at his shoes.

"Did you obliterate your wheels? *Shit, woman!*" The girl stings the scalp bad and he says something I do not hear. "What?"

The hangdog speaks up. "Repossessed."

"Bowtie you are a hopeless son of a bitch." Bowtie is clicking his heel on the cement of the floor and wipes his forehead. He clearly is in need of some direction so I say, "Find Philly."

The girl says, "What in God's name did he do to your head, Acie?"

Bowtie, man with a plan. "I talked to Marva last night and she said Philly left there after supper." Philly's friend Marva is another nut roll. We had some history. Two nights twenty years back.

"Fuck her," I say. "Bricks."

"What?" says Bowtie.

"Bricks on my head, a brick."

Florence Nightingale stops the daubing. "Like a noogie?" she says. Crazy chicklet. "A what?"

Bowtie looks up at me under his hat. "He rubbed your head with a brick?"

"Jesus. Jesus, Acie," the girl goes. "Now hold still." Every move she makes smarts my braincase. "I've got to cut away some of this other hair or the rest won't heal. Do you have any scissors?"

"Fuck all this," I say and rise up. The whole aggrieved enterprise burns on my head like acid. Fuck the all.

{

Bowtie goes to do his show. The girl agrees after some wheedling to get me my provisions and I keep the gate locked while she is gone. I have myself all the daily pills and a few more for the extra pain and I try to see if my piss gland works and when it does not I try to lie on my setup but there is no position where I am not downwind of agony.

What do I care what he is into and who knows it. Or what Philomena Stevenson has in her sleeve. She could be Mama in *Cleopatra Jones*, or Doodlebug angling to independ. My own brother could have been Beetle promising to be my man so that I will soon be eating lizards live in the desert to my self survive after his betrayal. They all may have stepped on some considerable toes without a care to who pays and *who pays* is me. My thought is to feed Bowtie to the lions so they slink off content.

Maybe if I rest the back of my head in a half sit.

Then I am moving the pillow and underneath the gun, and there is no gun. *Bowtie! Bastard!* and I am saying it out loud.

She thinks perhaps this cottage cheese is spoiled. She has ordered the dieter's plate and the meat patty, too, does not look right.

At the next booth over, a colored man with his back to her sips from a cup and his white companion bites into a BLT. She used to be able to eat bacon, she thinks, and remembers her husband's aversion. He would not have ordered a BLT, nor would he have gone out for a social lunch with a colored man.

The waitress hurries by her. "Miss!" she calls. "This potted cheese is spoiled!"

Waitress doesn't even nod. The old woman thinks leaving no tip will serve that waitress right, acting like she's too good for me.

Cindy

Only when I left the store did my shock register. I was out of it, moving out of habit alone, here but not here. First *Harnett*—it hadn't sunk in, Acie his father, Acie calling him *Bowtie,* Harnett's not telling me when I had asked about the store. And then Acie, this man with his miniature dog, his friend Wyans and his Colt, involved in something that would abrade his skull and plaster into his blood the oily strands of what remained of his hair.

It was something seedy, unbelievable: the scene like WPA murals of the jitterbugging hordes, Studs Lonigan's lost Chicago, Sister Carrie's fall into desperate straits. The Invisible Man, stringing his fest lights, fixing himself up.

It was exhausting, acting like I had seen this kind of thing before. School. Classes. Where was my center of gravity? It was up to me to walk away, and I *could,* in a minute—I'd just get him his malt liquor and I'd go.

Harnett had been changed, smaller, a peon, sitting on the concrete beside Acie's filthy stove, letting Acie harangue him, not bright, loquacious, instructive, smooth. Knowing he clerked in the Bebop

Shop, even assistant manager, diminished him, the Bebop catering to the squirrelly "buffs." Harnett now preoccupied by his morning show, the el ride to Evanston, the LPs he had in hand. Shaking his head, as I did, when Acie closed the door, saying not to worry, all was okay, he'd find his aunt Philomena and they'd sort out the story, but he was looking away, his mind elsewhere, on the outside, his sleek, smart self, ducking his good-bye.

"Why didn't you tell me?" I'd asked.

"And have you think I'd be looking like that? No way."

Now with Acie's list in hand, in snow.

I had gone shopping for Mom, weekends in college, out Receda Boulevard, to Ralph's Safeway in the old Falcon, stopping on the way with my own LP list. "Indulging yourself again?": her thanks, my reward. *Better for you than vodka sours and Carltons:* I preferred the liquor without the mixer even then.

State Street whirled in snow, traffic on Chicago Avenue a whisper far off, a car rolling down State sounding like someone slowly ripping velvet. Walgreen's six or eight blocks up Rush Street for the ointment and gauze, across the street from it a market where Acie had told me to find a Miss Nancy to give me the malt liquors, Sunday package goods and blue laws aside.

Snow like this only happened on *Wagon Train.* Falling on me like the disconnectedness I felt, a sense that I was as uninhabited as the plaster "tourists" under the stairs at the Museum of Contemporary Art. What was I doing, roving for *wound dressings?* Acie, alone behind lock, key, grate; his humoring me week after week, what did I do to his business? But what *is* his business?

Me, somebody *else's* "other." And suddenly, out of the pit of me, the wetness rising to meet the wet snow on my face, I was crying, sobbing, all of Chicago a whirl of white and I a speck in the middle of it. If I dissolved, no one would know—Acie would only want his supplies, Harnett would shrug and hit on someone else, my mother pour another drink. And Bobbi? Or my "boyfriend"? California, a life lived in the predictable morass of my mother's house, glamour of my boyfriend's crowd, seemed like someone else's life, an illusory scrim over a blank, edgeless white. I had thrown it all away just to leave home and who anyway gave a fuck about art?

Out of the snow, whirling, suddenly: Harnett, doubled-back.

"Girl." Close enough to see my face, my eyes then. "Oh girl. Come on there." His collar up, his hat, shoulders white. "You okay?"

He ducked me toward a building, a dry cleaners' door. In the slight space of the doorway, his breath on my face.

"Why aren't you doing your show?"

He ignored this. "There, girl. It'll be all right." His eyes were focused not on mine but on some far point. "You know I need to talk to you."

"You know what's going on? With Acie?"

"There." He was looking straight at me now; it felt unusual. "We could use your help, girl." He pushed a limp strand of my hair back under my hat. "Have been meaning to ask you, just waiting for the right time." I said nothing, listening, feeling the wet chill now of my jeans, my boots. "Girl, we've got some art we've got to, I've got to move, and those collectors you know, if you—"

"Art?" Vertigo. "You have to move some art?"

"Sell, you know. If you could set up a meeting, or—"

"What kind of art?"

"Paintings, shit—" and he was looking at me, then away, taking a breath, "we'll talk later, girl. I got to go do this show." He cupped my head and my hat in his hand and kissed my forehead. "Can't go into the whole thing now, just think about it. Don't mention it to my dad."

A man my age with a large, bounding dog passed us. A normal man. Wearing hand-knit mittens and a snowflake sweater, hiking boots under jeans, smiling, laughing, calling "Cricket" to the dog, laughs muted by the snow. In half a block the street swallowed him.

Harnett's face expectant, wet.

"I'm just a student—" I thought of Professor Bartel, his Dada lectures, I thought of my Chinese survey class, pages of bronze vessels with wave-like patterns. Certain students who seemed rich. I should walk away, I thought.

No Water Tower Place, no Arby's even, the white a siege. Disappearing ahead, out the door of the Walgreen's: someone so much like my boss Simone that for a moment I wanted to call to her. Couldn't be. Glare in car lights, wet boots.

"I'll see you later. It's all going to be all right, girl." And he was gone.

"The way Glenn Miller played, na na na the hit parade, those were the days," and then, switch: "Ford Pinto trial update and the Shah of Iran, on the move, news at noon."

Acie locked the gate behind me, I took the soggy bag to the back room, the TV so loud I had to hit the window through the grate with one of the cans of pork and beans. The dog and her raspy yelps, bolting for the back room when she saw me.

"What are you watching?" Keep it offhand so he won't think you'll linger to watch with him. Just see that he's safe and mending and leave.

No answer.

"In other news, a sleeping giant has awakened. The long-dormant volcano Mount St. Helens on the Oregon-Washington state border erupted last night, spewing . . ."

"Where's the Colt?"

Waving him aside, pulling from the middle of the bag a smaller bag. He took two cans to the mattress with him, opening one, bent over the aerial on the junky TV; I wanted the third, resisted, internally arguing it, leaving it bagged but ready. When Acie was satisfied with the picture he lay down, grunting as his head hit the pillow. The dog by the sink, her snout on her forefeet, popping her nervous eyes back and forth as I unpacked the groceries.

"President Carter has signed the 1980 Refugee Act, allowing 30,000 additional refugees entrance to the U.S. each year."

Acie grunted. "Pecker."

Needing to pee, had wanted to go to Arby's while out, too much wind and snow for the extra block but Acie's toilet stall without a door, no light either, no door. He couldn't see anything from the bed. "Acie, don't get up. I have to pee."

A pause, mumbling. "My head is not raising itself just because your pants will be falling." The dog's worried eyes on my shoes.

It's probably best not to see what's in here. No lid on the toilet, how does he shit? I hovered, peed, tried to find toilet paper without touching a surface, settled for drip-dry. Leaning against the stall wall, beside the toilet, what looked like picture frames poking through a tear in Kraft paper wrapping.

My curiosity overcame my stomach. They'd been peeing on this when they missed the bowl. I picked it up. Gingerly, not rattling.

Half dark. Two frames. One ornate, chipped at the corner, set with glass; beneath the glass a pen and ink drawing of two figures huddled by the sea, a fish standing on its tail, looming over them. Acie rustled, shifting on the bed. The figures' outlines were firmly drawn in ink but filled with dry, scratchy hatchings and lines.

The other frame, plain slatting, coated with a black worn thin in spots, and a painting the size of a sheet of typing paper. Black outlines, saturated color, hewn shapes unlike Chagall's or Rouault's, the style resembling—

"You fall in?"

Max Beckmann's. Both.

Flushing, trying to put them back in place without the paper making noise, partly succeeding.

Art in Acie's toilet to "move."

And Harnett looking for collectors. And not Romare Bearden, Betye Saar. Not even Chicago's own Richard Hunt.

Max Beckmann. What were the chances?

Acie's eyelids closed. "I hate to ask, Acie, but that was the rest of my cash," I said.

And why was it sitting next to the toilet, just left around?

He didn't look up from a commercial for Donahue. "I will resupply you before you leave." The dog stood on the bed beating her tiny tail against his hip.

For a moment I was close to asking about the paintings, but then didn't. "Well, how about now? I was thinking I'd take off."

Acie focused on the television, not moving his abraded head.

I waited. Din of an investment commercial. I raised my voice.

"Acie, you okay? I'll need to be going." Too solicitous and he would take it as patronizing. I didn't know how he lost his eye, I didn't know what he did under his pinups, alone, I didn't know how many Colt 45s he packed away in a day or what other Colts he packed, I didn't know what he was doing with *Brücke* paintings and why someone took a brick to his scalp. This cash was meant for drinks.

"Girl," suddenly, pretending he had dozed off and awakened.

"How long is Harnett's show?"

"Not for you to be thinking about, Florence Nightingale. You go." He winced raising himself from the pillow, the dog lifted her head. "I will get you your ends."

I hoped he meant my money. He did, two twenties, his pleather purse.

"It wasn't that much, Acie."

"Time to go," giving me a backhand wave.

Suddenly a loud whistle screeching from the store, a drumming, a noise like a xylophone—deafening, earsplitting. "Jesus!" By the time I found I'd jumped, orienting, I heard the toy trumpet, knew it was the Art Ensemble of Chicago's "Live from Mandel Hall," loud as a jackhammer. Against the music, the dog's yips sounded like machine guns on helium.

Acie shot through the beaded curtain, his voice railing in the dinning mix of television and the Art Ensemble. Through the curtain I saw Harnett, inside the front door, squinting up at a corner mirror and a looping light while Acie pointed toward a cord that ran from a small box on the wall. A bleat from Lester Bowie's trumpet bending in the tinny speakers.

"—the switch at the setup," Acie was yelling to me. I found a light switch on the wall beside the curtain and flicked it.

"It's A-a-a-a-lbert!" The television, blaring now, seemed like peace itself.

But the noise had animated Acie. He smiled genially, regaining his broad, cantankerous power beside his son, Harnett looking green in the fluorescence, the dog at his side still yipping.

"What happened to your show?" Asking this because Acie didn't. Acie pulled the box's cord on the wall gently to the left, aligning it with something only he saw.

"You two," he said, "do not seem to be appreciating an invention of genius. But you will be." Pointing at the mirrors in the four corners of the room, a new man now, demonstrating an invention, a product. "That is the laser you foisted upon my self," he said to Harnett. "And that noise is what those mock natives—" interrupting himself, verbiage smitten, "you acquainted with the mock turtle soup?—the mock natives and their musics are tailor made for."

Harnett's nose flared, hard. "I called Stamper to fill in and came back, it's brutal out there," Harnett said, Acie stopping, looking at him, arms crossed, scalp gummed up again in a kind of red, globby sheen.

Acie's good eye glued on Harnett. Thirst. I wanted to go.

"Well, this girl was just leaving herself, and you can be too, soon as I have a word with you." But they were both between me and the door, Acie not moving, seeming to forget me as soon as he'd spoken, so I backed up behind the beaded curtain into his room, Acie's voice beginning to rumble in the background, I afraid to sit on the floor (dirt, bugs, dark) so standing and watching the Fat Albert cartoon, waiting to hear a lull in the outer room.

Both Acie's and Harnett's voices urgent, rising then falling. A commercial, "Ask Mikey!"—then another, blaring a car, then a network spot for *The White Shadow* and his basketball team. Suddenly Acie drew the curtain, both he and Harnett coming in, making the air electric, charged, with a gun Acie held in his hand.

"Stay a little longer, girl," Acie drawled, calm, smiling, suddenly healed of pain and large, looming. He raised the gun toward me, looking not at it but at me with his left eye, and then tilted it away from me so that I could see the side of it. "Safety catch is on now, so you can cool your konk." Still looking at me, his saying, "I am grateful to have this back."

Why did I stay? Why did I stay at home and commute, for that matter, through college, even though the loan officer had asked about a dorm, why did I stay in graduate school knowing by now the field wasn't mine? Why had I gone to all those meetings and then pulled out the bottle in the car afterwards anyway? No day at a time, no detach with love, just hour by hour detaching, without. Did I really think Acie would shoot the gun to keep me there? No.

"Glad you like Chicago XOXO Bobbi." I'd finally gotten mail, scrawled, a postcard of a painting of a boy by Bronzino, haughty, disdainful, pinky ringed. Sleek as a seal. I could have left.

He was settling in, seizing the skanky mattress again, pontificating. Rat-infested shithole. Blowhard. De-magnetize me.

"The '38 Jamboree was a pretty sight."

Two hours of Acie holding forth, regaling, all the time in the world, not a care, his speech hepper than usual, tiresome, scary. Weird shit, the saying went: Acie lying on his bed with a gun on his stomach, Harnett shifting side to side, about to blow: the dynamics, the gun, tension, paralysis. I felt invisible, but the show Acie made of disinterest in Harnett was almost demonic.

"A jam it was the New Century Committee threw us on three stages, black, white, a roll. Konks so plentiful they gave out the gates, and me and Redd, you remember Redd Fox, don't you, Bowtie, me, and Redd waltzed ourselves right in."

Acie patted the gun.

"Now the Regal Theater was one luxe crib, and the Sherman had the history with the black-like-me's, but the Club DeLisa had to be my ballroom of choice."

A long history lesson, endless, rambling, not unlike the lessons I got from Harnett, the son now standing by the back window, looking out at dirt-level, not ten feet away. The one overhead bulb made

Harnett look even slighter than he was, his overcoat off, a vest over his T-shirt. He rolled his eyes at me, then looked again at the back lot. "The revolution that was bop mind you. Negroes was not free to enter El Grotto until '44.

"The Pres played the Regal, he played the Savoy, he played the DeLisa, and they were all sellout shows in this town. But the recording was happening in New York." Acie paused. The dog on her back beside him with her miniature belly in the air.

"See the slave masters there coveted the souls of the players, because left to their own resources they were naturally without souls of their own."

I leaned against the sink, checking first for bugs. A wave of Harnett and his smooth skin—I knew that whatever was going on had little to do with this monologue, but at last, worn through, I'd exhausted fear, thirsty. I wanted to distract Acie, break the spell. "So did you ever record?" My voice cracking.

Harnett shifted impatiently, his mouth shut, still not looking at Acie reclining on the mattress with the gun in his pants.

"That phone plugged in?" Harnett suddenly asked, Acie turning his head toward him in an exaggerated manner, I knowing it must hurt his scalp, scraping the pillow in its festering state, then turning back. Even a beer.

"Not in a serious manner," Acie, to me. "You needed capital."

On cue, the telephone: ringing.

Acie in his bloody mohawk still calm, in charge. The receiver. "Well. We have been wondering where you got to. Your nephew looking for you high and low." He listened, and with the television down I could hear the agitated, haranguing pitch of a woman's voice fall from the phone. "No, last thing you need now is coming around here. If the—" He stopping, raising the eyebrow over the glass eye to me, suddenly seeing me.

"Do not you rattle their cage," he said, finally. "Stay yourself clear and you will be all right." A pause, more harangue. "All right. You call a car to get you there, now where are you now." Suddenly I noticed Harnett listening to him intently, leaning in with his kufi, tilted from the window frame. Just the breeze of another voice, a phone call, had made me feel my shoulders again, the tension lowering a degree, reminder there was an *outside*. Boots still damp and cold. Yards away, paintings by a toilet.

"Seeing you then—" Acie closing his eyes for a moment, listening, then his mouth moving. Let me out, give me a drink.

"That woman walks with a force field," Acie said, hanging up, moving the gun on his chest, regarding his son for a long moment. "But if she does, you are the Darth Vader."

Harnett staring back at his father. Overwhelming, the need for air.

"Could I put some music on, Acie?" Harnett looked away then, but Acie still pinned him in place with his eye.

"Do that, girl. You know Cy Touff is back around town. Why don't you see what we got of his." The dog's head perking up.

The store seemed a cavernous paradise after a few hours in the back room, its strung bulbs brighter, the rows of standing bins and the shelved boxes overhead ordered, reassuring, neat, but Cy Touff had no bin that I could find. I could leave, walk out the door—cold, no coat—bass trumpet? Recorded with Nat Pierce? I tried to remember what I knew, distracted, listening still for a crash in the back room.

Suddenly, Acie, rustling through the beaded curtain. Carrying my coat, inexplicably hurried, the lazy front gone. "I thought you were going awhile back. Go on. Here is your coat."

Outside, it was still snowing, the descending sheet of it making a kind of glow in the darkening air, an Albert Pinkham Ryder painting, that eerie light he stretched over a nighttime landscape. I heard stray, muted traffic as I picked my way down toward the Loop, occasionally the sound of a snow shovel scraping concrete. The Loop's department stores were shut tight, a lone bus pulling away from the pedestrian mall on State Street. Office towers—the Standard Oil building, the old Monadnock, Illinois Centers One and Two—dark and sealed, street-level windows obsidian in the streetlamps.

I broke one of the twenties for a cup of coffee at a red hots stand and treated myself to the IC instead of the bus, trying to decide what drink it would be, a celebration, busting out, the train seeming suspended in gel as it clicked along its track by the lake, rounding its way to Hyde Park. Carl Sandburg's town it was, Grant Wood's, and I was still in it. Fortune was mine for a lesson.

"I didn't tell you about Harold's lambasting Bilandic on his own patch?" Clarence spoons the potatoes out of the bowl for Ruthie.

"He made it ahead of Bilandic to his own news conference, just walked right up to the rostrum afore Mayor Bilandic got his self there." Clarence can still laugh thinking of it. Ruthie scowls, pushing him with her hip to the end of the table so he'll stop slopping the potatoes about. He drops the spoon distractedly as he moves, smiling.

"Harold called Bilandic a third-rate Daley. He said he had all of Daley's weak qualities and none of his good; unable, Harold said, to get a consensus out of two white-sheeters in a race riot. You never seen anything like it! Midway through," and here Clarence stops and blows his nose in a handkerchief, burying his big glasses, "police sergeant got up and turned off the mike, but Harold keep reading from his statement cool as a cucumber."

"Since you are speaking of cucumbers," says Ruthie, "go wash yourself up."

Acie

Bowtie. The runt is keen on my midsection once I get the gun back. This worrying of his to keep track of it riles me the most.

Bowtie's ma dunked him to a name like an English throne-warmer. It did not take me long to find him one more fitting, as from the time he was a crumb-crusher he had aspirations to the high life.

He is accessorized. He stands up there by the platter spinner in the kufi and the coat and the briefcase. She raised him a pretender and now I can see the fruits of his usurpation. I raise up the gun.

"And how did this happen to get into your pocket?"

"Acie, I'm just in a corner here. I've got a lot of safety concerns right now."

"*Safety concerns?* What in everloving do you got going? Do not bring your *safety* concerns in *my* proximity!"

"Acie—" A whiner also.

"Go on. Get yourself to the crib and we will have us a percolator."

"What?" He looks at me with all of the malice that that mother of his could breed.

"It is too late to instruct you in your own tongue. Go on." The curtain parts, the girl like a bent banana looks up and moves herself over.

"Stay a little longer, girl," I say and show her the gun lock. And then I start up my show. My music-enlightenment show. The show where I show you to be aberration and abomination. No son of mine.

When the presentation for the lovebirds starts to wind down and I give the girl a boot, before I turn off the TV I head out front with a purpose. Miles Dewey Davis did his fusion-confusion gig at the Auditorium awhile back, man in a white visor and a white jacket, now that was a way with accessories, Miles looking that night to be Spy versus Spy. Backstage recording of this gig came my way so I put the pressing onto the turntable for the aggravation of my son and I head back to the crib.

Cut I cue is the hand drummer. Young upstart believes himself to be sliced bread so Miles lets him fury himself on the tom-toms and bongos for a full five minutes while he himself checks out the ceiling. This is what I do with my own usurper. I pee and putter carefree with Bowtie worrying himself at attention.

When Davis back onstage he inclined his horn and a cool two bleats is what it took to show up the drummer and his conflagration, and this is loud and clear on the recording. Upstart got whittled right on the spot. After the show I saw Davis backstage but he has been way too good for Acie Stevenson for years. Since Bowtie's ma was a bone of contention.

My own two bleats are concerning the girl.

"Girl a high pixie." I act like Bowtie is hardly present.

"Un hunh."

"Clean up good though."

Bowtie. Ready your self.

"My Tie." It sounds like *My Lai* and I say it again to remind this spring-off of my own of a bad war. I was too flat-footed when my time had come, but they could not find a qualifying flaw on Bowtie despite the legion I instructed him to recount. "You got words for your self?"

That my fish made *him*. Bowtie is so worked up he has chewed his cheek half away. Miles's backup does the driving sludge up from the bass section.

"Sorry I borrowed the gun."

I hit him once when he was small, I tried it on but it did not fit.

"Did my ears hear something?"

"Sorry I took the gun, Acie, there's been a lot going down, and out on the street without a car and . . . sorry."

He squints and my head blazes. "Who do you *got* on your tail? Who on the road, for example? If you are messing with the medicine you are gone, you are on your own."

Now he looks away. That my fish made a weasel. A guitar run comes on and I do not mind saying that this rockification was the Miles's worst move ever.

This the last hesitation I will be bearing. What we have is one Iguana man, dashiki head bricking me, Miss Philly puling on the phone lines, and the offspring of my own dick in dissemblement before me. The Colt can has left my hand and before Bowtie can move, it catches him in the chest hard and the can hits before him on the cement and sloshes its containments at his trousers. "What the fuck!" The Bow Tie acts surprised. Why am I going through this information session in my crib when I do not get information?

"How were you knowing the white girl?"

"I *told* you already. We met at a club."

"What were you doing at your Willy's?"

"I was in New York! He was my uncle!" Here is a boy who I never knew not scamming and he just a good nephew.

"Remind me again. Why were you in New York?"

"I went for The Hymen!" This is what Bowtie calls his boss at my competition, the respect he shows. "We've been *through* this, Acie. It was an industry trip."

"Industry? Since when does he do more than humor up to the one stops?" He may run a white operation over at the Bebop Shop but not that white. He is not up sending the dregs of Bowtie out to New York City for him. And all he features is local. That cacophony by The Association for the Advancement of Cornrow Musicians.

Over Bowtie's head the flakes in the high windows just make a spark on the corner of my icebox. I need to get to the throne and a marijuana cigarette would be helpful to my head.

"Ask Philly."

A loopy droopy head, Bowtie. "What?"

"I can't *tell* you. You should ask Philly, you're going to be seeing her, right?"

Take the cake. "You cannot tell me, but the missing queen, no blood relation of mine or yours, is supposed to fill me in? Is she on the horse, too?"

I got a pharmacist for a son but apparently not a successful one on account he has here both repossession *and* trouble.

"What?" There is no reaction from my son the Barrymore.

"More than a Colt is going to be flying your way."

"No one's on the horse."

"I begot you, I can break you."

He drops the act and now he is just humoring his progenitor. "Listen, Acie, I will not take the gun again and I will do whatever you want and I will get Philly to talk to you but fuck just lay off. I've *told* you I can't tell you."

"I will do you one better," I say. I am fed up with my own fish and what they concocted in the womb of that bitch. "Get your own lying self off." And then I grab his arm and push him out through the beads

and the bins and I unlock the front and undo the grate with Bowtie
ventilating concerning his coat I got inside and the snow. But he is out
in it and by any account it slowed up a while ago. I do not even look
to see if the Iguana himself is there to pluck the fruit off of my mighty
tree. Come and get him, do me the favor, Brotherman.

⟨

Blisters on the feet can really ice a cake that already feels the effects of an internal collapse. This is why from November on I tend to stay in.

Tonight I have no choice in the matter, so with the head in mullah wraps and boats on the feet it is looking more likely I will be experiencing blisters before the evening is out. The world does not give up.

Why she chose that spaghetti house the Como Inn has no reason except to make me pay. In the door I am cased and the telephone is employed and another of the mob brothers comes down the back stairs that have got velvet on them for carpet and asks me, if I am a man of the cloth. I say a revelation fell on me, which he can take in his own way but I know it is true which brings me a smile in a tiresome situation. The penguins give me back my social security card and tell me to enjoy the food, Mullah Stevenson. I do not plan on it.

She is tucked back behind the greenery but I hear her plain as day. It is an island bar in a dark room supposing to spell glamour to the uninitiated and so justify a five-dollar libation. Turns out a piano singer like Perry Como is employed at the Como Inn and at this moment he is attempting "Moonlight in Vermont."

"He just has a weight problem is all," is what I hear her announcing to the continent, then I hear her and another female do the woman hoot and then the other one says, "A weight problem! A truck got no problem parking in *his* garage!" The place is doing a big Sunday business but the Philly show carries over the entire shebang.

Philomena's acquaintance from the projects. Woman I had the misfortune to romance when the liquor overrode my good sense.

"Acie, you say hello to Marva."

"Marva," I say. Marva has a hat with a high net fan on its top.

"Acie," says Marva. She and Miss Philly could have the plus sizes all sewn up.

"What is sitting on your head, Acie Stevenson? You a Islam brother now?" says Philly.

She motions to the cocktail waitress and wiggles her finger across the table to indicate she wants her and Marva set up again, and the waitress looks at me for my own order when Marva says, "Oh no, Philly. I'll be going now." Then she turns to me. "I was just keeping her company until you got here." Huh. I see dollars when I see the evidence of them, and here there are not only full mixed drinks but plates indicating a food order. She will not be leaving the green to cover, either, we know this. A malt liquor is not a selection and so I order a Bud on tap.

Marva is extricating herself from her chair which may be a lasting project. Philly does not look the worse for her alleged wear but it is difficult to tell in the lights dim for the mob molls.

"I asked you, Acie, what is that headpiece?"

I do not answer again but take in the full Marva showing all the signs of buttering both sides of her bread. She used to be on the shorn side. "See you later, honey," she says not to me and she goes.

"Just had a talk with your nephew."

Philly does not seem to care. Alone, she gives up on my hat and changes her tack but I still do not get answers to my questions. "Even Marva's place in the projects is consi*de*rably more comfortable than your mangy hotel."

I make apparent my considerable lack of interest.

"You can be telling me what you got in store with the Bowtie."

Miss Philly shoots a look. "As soon as Harnett fixes up some business he's been helping us with, you won't hear any more of it."

"Helping *us?* You and your larva Marva?"

The waitress sits down a pink drink in front of Philly. The glass she gives to me would not quench a mosquito.

"Acie, your brother had an enterprise on the side, but it is no concern of yours." Hincty bitch. If this is what the widow does, then save me from having myself one.

"*William?*" I do not remember the brother pushing the powder.

"It does not concern you."

The boy and the woman were invented to punish me for my excesses. "You and the ingrate have in*vade*d my concerns. With your *bus*iness." I nod the headdress at her.

Philly does her snort. Before you get to the widow, you have to endure the woman.

"Enterprise needs to reveal itself or you and the usurper will be banned from the Palace." White girl's own double-cross eating at me, the Bowtie and her involved, too. "You, the runt, and the chippy."

Bowtie and Philly should start a road show. Master Barrymore and Miss Bernhardt. "Chippy. What chippy?"

"You did not answer my question, woman."

"Why should I? Harnett is old enough to have and mind his own business, and you are barking up the wrong tree, Acie, as usual. What happened to you and that helmet you got on your head?"

"Your *business* associate came by for the innocent. The old Iguana to the Palace." She looks off fogged.

The management comes to the door of the bar like they are a pack of dogs sniffing hindquarters, and I weigh asking Miss Philly more questions. I am sick of getting no answers from the Relations Troupe.

"No one is lifting a finger on behalf of you or the offspring until further information is furnished."

She says nothing so I change my tack.

"I know the Bowtie came by you in August."

She looks to be reflecting on this. "You have you a good son, Acie, the Lord knows how. He's a striver for betterment, and you could take a tip from him."

"One way or another *some*body got him in the medicine and now you say the somebody was my brother."

"*Your* boy? He doesn't do nothing serious." Her head goes to its side again. "Acie, William was only trying to keep us in food and hot water."

She looks at me implacable.

"You lay on me how he got started at it."

She begins to fan herself with the drink card from the table.

There is a rustle at the door to the room and through the foliage I see the spice increase with the entrance of Washington. He was a runt when I was ahead of him in school but he is my size now, and he has an entourage more smiley than himself. I have heard around that he cannot get enough of the capos bringing him his salad forks at this Como Inn and now the hobnobber with the mobbers is live and in person. Washington sweeps the whole room for a far table and I know when he passes the jungle, I in my turban will stand out. I am right.

"Acie Stevenson!" He has his girth in a suit so he makes sure to use it shaking hands.

"Washington."

"Sorry I was to hear about William. May the Lord keep him close." He has himself a manner and a face that may bring us some luck yet.

"Thank you."

"You have the better company tonight, Acie," he says turning the gentleman manner on Philly. His men stand back. "Harold Washington, honored to make your acquaintance."

"Philomena Stevenson. Pleased to meet *you*." The cones on her chest increase their circumference.

"William was always the cutup in class that kept the rest of us honest," Washington is saying. "How is your mother bearing up?"

"Passed three years back."

"Oh, I am sorry to hear that, Acie." He shifts the weight and makes to edify the entourage. "Acie's mother was an artist, an intelligent woman—there was no one sharper than Mrs. Stevenson, in this city then or now—and she was a caring woman with a fine sense of discretion and the fortitude to shoulder others' burdens along with her own. I would have wanted to be present at her services, Acie; I regret missing her passing."

I do not tell him the services were myself making payment for the mortuary to fit her out in the plot beside Hezekiah without my involvement before William could get in and make himself a production of it. "She always kept her eye on you, Washington."

He takes his time, unlike his men that are shifting to be done with me. "How's business on the North Side? I should come by—I've been wanting to pick up that new Milt Hinton."

"Keeps me in headgear."

This gets his amusement and a smile large as the entourage. "I wasn't going to comment, Acie, but that is one arresting bonnet."

"Arrest*ed* is what it's going to get him," chimes in Philly beside herself.

"Thirty years of service to the Shriners," I say, and Washington really likes this one. He always was quick.

"Just don't fall asleep at a meeting," he says chuckling and lays a hand on my shoulder. "Be seeing you. We could use your sense."

"What's he?" Philly whispers loud as the Washington swarm moves off.

"Looking to be congressman," I say, "now that he has got the credentials."

The Philly-face is blank as the desert. She clearly does not know politics in Chicago so I spell it out.

"Jail."

Back and in the crib, my head thinks it will take on the job of a kettle-drum. I lock and alarm the Palace and think I will rest up the hammering on the pillow and then investigate the Doc band on the *Tonight Show* but in a wink I see Redd Fox and me out celebrating my turning seventeen like we did in the armory and it is the night Joe Louis takes heavyweight champion of the world. On the considerable stage Roy Eldridge blows the Goodman off the roof and Truck Parham plucks catgut like twat. Before my mind gets around the ropes up above a white head swings in my view followed by a white fist. My scalp ignites itself and I got two orange butterflies ringing it, then it turns out the flappers are after the molasses that is what is stinging my head. The crowd roars up for Roy but it is Benny Goodman at the top, and he opens with Jelly's "King Porter Stomp," but the Goodman is the Iguana and he takes off from the stage with the butterflies behind him, giant, and Sally Rand naked in her feather fans brings up the rear, and just like on the nervous chippy in the bird movie they dive on me with their pecking-beaks, at me to empty the tray under my ma's icebox like they are employed by her. I know I got to wash my head off, clean the bird shit off and the molasses, detach myself out from the Braddock fist still over my ear. Redd laughs like a bird. He says, "You sure got some bad flavors in your mouth!" but it is Bowtie saying this and I think to myself it has been a time since I have seen Bowtie laughing. He throws his drink square in my face and pants—missing my midsection—and I look around for Sally Rand. She has taken up french kissing the Dinah at the bar, but the Dinah slaps her and turns to me now stamping her foot. "Acie, fuck you, you milkpot!" She makes a dramatic exit and I wonder if the milkpot refers to my wet dick.

The baggie is bust. The dog Ma got her scratchy pimento tongue at my face and she is putting all her juice to it. Art Ensemble nightmare blasting.

I got the gun. Not a moving shadow in the crib. Nothing out of the front room, but the noise would drown it. I throw the light and my rigged alarm switch at the beads and then drop my considerable pounds. From my perch on the floor there is nothing, only sound of wind with the cool blast in through an open door.

"Don't shoot, Acie!"

The offspring.

"I got nowhere else at the moment. *Please* let me stay with you."

Chris Evert steps onto the selling floor at Marshall Field's, Water Tower Place, and a glow descends and follows her, like Tinkerbell's ball of light, as she threads through the cases. Downtown, on the twenty-sixth floor of Standard Oil, a secretary scrapes the last of her cole slaw from its takeout cup and turns a page of Ebony. *Farther south, a man steps out in the cold from the median on Stony Island Boulevard into the smack of a Toyota sedan. And along the 94 corridor past Gary and on toward Ohio, the space-station webs of industrial pipes and chutes emit their flames and their vapors. They condense in the afternoon sun.*

Cindy

For a while when I got back, sitting still, on my bed. The overhead in that room was bright, the dormitory floor lamp on its highest setting, nothing behind my reflection in the window but a swallowing black. Two buoyant voices in the hall outside my door approached each other, murmured and bubbled, lifted, receded. My boots, soaked through. Oh, poor *me*. Violins.

The reflection blurred the circles under my eyes but I still looked like shit, hat on, underneath it limp, dirty hair, an urchin, a witch. A girl in my Chinese bronzes class carried a Vuitton bag, with leather the color of butter and soft as cheese. Maybe I was hungry, maybe I just needed dairy. What I needed was another draft. Starting to warm.

Finally on my feet, at the window, is there anyone out there thinking of me, then: no you don't—go out. So the coat going on again, for Valois: See Your Food. I would. See my food. Steam tables for low-lifes like dad, my destiny, O She of Disability, too. Salisbury steak.

As for *you*, Jim Beam, so standup to fit the coat pockets of girls. Stepping out.

Then a resolve cemented in the night—whether I dreamed or just came to it, I wasn't sure. An urge for change, a sense of buckling down, knuckling under, committing myself to study and a new life. Scholarship and glamour. Suits cut like Berenson's, the art historian, from Italy. Along Fifty-seventh Street the snow sparkled in the coldest air yet, Regenstein Library gleaming like the monolith in *2001*, the guard waving me through, into the bright granite space, glistening with endeavor. I shook my head and my hair moved, clean.

Shower, makeup, making me more art historian than Acie.

Whatever city this was, I was stuck here, as I was stuck in art history, but there were fates that were worse. I'd study, excel, not drink before six; in the light-studded skyline my own lamp would bleat. My mother, Bobbi, Harnett—I'd need none of them, and what new friends I'd make would need *me*.

With the reserve reading I staked myself in one of the deep armchairs in front of the windows. From there I could see high cirrus wisps dotting the sky over the lakefront on the South Side, ice too cold to melt shimmering in the sun on the parapets of the campus buildings.

Page 149 in the Herschel Chipp: it was Nolde. Print before me imprinting, the task before me a gift, a bounty, *to read.*

> Relatives of my father's visited me one evening. Pious as in a church, shyly and reluctantly they sat in front of *The Last Supper* and *The Pentecost.* The paintings moved them with their sacredness. "There is Christ, in the middle, and there is John, and this is probably Peter?" they asked, pointing to *The Last Supper.* "And who is sitting in the middle here?" they asked, looking to *The Pentecost.* When I said it was Peter, they became very quiet. If Peter looked like that during the Last Supper, he could not have another face in the Pentecost. One of these could not be true. —Such were their orientation and criticism.

Usually the religious reference, the arcane Bible stories and apocrypha I didn't know, something as simple as a mention of "Pentecost" dulled the rest, tuned me out. But in my new life, Nolde's complaints about family, about expectations of depiction, of type, the worried strangers about him—these leapt from the page to my head. A self-portrait from a lithograph faced the text, only one eye visible under the brim of a wide hat, the other somewhere in the shadow. Nolde had a mustache, seemed to hold a pipe.

In his own diaries Max Beckmann had written, "Nolde considers himself a genius, isn't one, and nonetheless wants to be treated as such."

But Nolde had called Beckmann an arrogant *Jugendliche*. Arrogant youth—Bobbi's postcard, the Bronzino boy. The figures in Nolde's paintings shared with Beckmann's a sense of absolute isolation.

The sky knotted in the distance, a darker hue; as I watched, it shifted again, just a sun with intermittent clouds.

"Mom?" The wall of the phone booth embellished with "Booty by Stephen Call x56112." In a tondo.

"Wait." I heard her turn down the Vic Damone. "What?"

"How are you?"

"You called to find out how I am?"

So a bad idea.

"Yes."

"What's wrong?"

I could call this Stephen and have my booty done. A better idea.

"Nothing, just wanted to call. How are you?"

She pausing, weighing my words, I could almost hear the scale bang with the weight on INSINCERE. "Can't complain." I did hear, loudly, clearly, ice clinking near the receiver.

"It's about eight in the morning there, isn't it?"

She knew what I meant. The first show by a Chicago artist I saw in Chicago, by Ray Yoshida, included a painting called *Unreliable Refuge,* the tentacular "Mom" and "Dad" striking above the "boy" and "girl" with knived protuberances, the boy turned to face the girl and the girl to face the viewer, her own tentacles folded in self-protection or prayer. The ground around the figures sizzled with specks. I shouldn't have started.

"You voted for this stupid sonofabitch."

"Mom—" And I could see her, ringed with light in the California kitchen, still in her lounging robe, circling the liquid in her glass with her tiny wrist and blowing smoke rings, steamed over Jimmy Carter. "Mom. I'll talk to you later."

"I won't hold my breath." And then, as evidence, she inhaled and exhaled audibly. I could taste the smoke. "Bye, dear."

"Bye."

Same cirrus, same sky, same parapets below. Nolde, Beckmann. *I'll look at a few.* The want of a drink, mosquito at my ear.

What was cool, bright in the study room now was cool and dark, industrial feeling, in the stacks, the metal shelves careening toward high, skinny windows slit into the cement, the fluorescent fixtures audible in the still. No whiskey now. Wait. The painting in Acie's bathroom—an odd, dark figure in a door; a footbridge; a huge empty ball in the center of the canvas where usually painters put their pyrotechnics—had had a crudeness to it, like Rouault's figures, or akin to Philip Guston's after his shift, Guston's giant stubbed cigarettes clumsy and dissettling on a painting's horizon. The other, the drawing of the vertical fish, had seemed out of a postcard, a fish story, but with the same distinct lines.

The Beckmann monographs: paintings, drypoints, lithographs, even a cast bronze sculpture of a woman crouching with one leg pushed back and up, her toes curling toward the top of the picture. "Take long walks and take them often," from a lecture he gave in 1948, "and try your utmost to avoid the stultifying motor car, which robs you of your vision, just as the movies do, or the numerous motley newspapers."

A painting: *Young Men by the Sea,* one sitting and two standing men flanking a figure of ambiguous sex, with a kind of toga draping its body, long hair, its arms braided across a chest. Unlike at Acie's, it wasn't a fish. Fish filled other paintings—*The Fisherwomen* in provocative dress kissing and holding their catch, while a hag stared glumly from behind them; *The Cabins,* a man struggling to carry a giant fish in front of stagey windows murky in the night; and a fish floating amid *The Artists with Vegetables* at their table. Then: *The Big Catfish.* 1929. In the black-and-white reproduction it even looked like Acie's drawing. Except here, there was a third figure.

The coolness of the stacks, my own back against the shelves, propping the book up on the shelf before me. Blood singing in its currents, iconography. Iconography, key—

A man with a lumberjack's bare arm squeezed the frame on three sides of the picture and held the fish upright, the fish's two eyes popping out at the viewer, its tail curling between the man's straddling legs, a woman to the right of them recoiling against a door (cabana? boat cabin?), eyes averted, hand out to stop the fish from swinging toward her.

The man blocked most of the view of a boat in full sail, only partially blocked the third figure over his shoulder: a woman with a parasol, hooded and cloaked, young, with bright, determined eyes fixed on the fish. The painting was square, 127 centimeters on each side, large.

I looked at the sizes of the other paintings. 173 × 125, 198 × 150, 208 × 99, the smallest 63 × 58. The painting at Acie's was smaller than these—maybe a foot and a half square, smaller even than the drawing sharing the same brown wrapping. And where were Beckmann drawings?—from the MOMA monograph to another, a German one, and under each reproduction of a sketch the German read "Radieren," *etching*. Neither text was indexed by medium, technique, so plate by plate, page by page, I checked each reproduction. Lots of paintings, lots of etchings. No drawings.

Me: a sleuth. Against the backdrop of, say, Sonny Rollins's "Freedom Now Suite," my act cleaned up, I would solve a major art-world mystery. Outside, the sky had darkened, suspended, pendulous, but the air was too cold for snow. Where to, now?

That night, studying, bright dorm overheads, just one beer.

"Cindy. It's Harnett."

Out of their lives—a moment it would take, I could put the receiver back and that would be that. Not answer when it rang again.
Instead, asking, hearing myself, "You okay?"

Acie had held the gun on his son. Now I sucked a paper cut while
I listened.

"Yeah, yeah, I'm fine. Acie was just messed up, don't worry. So did
you, you know, do you know anybody? Any collectors?"

I saw Acie looming in his aisle like a whale. Harnett, on the make,
harpooned by the fish in a terrible turn. "Why?" I asked.

"The pictures, my uncle's—trying to sell them for my aunt
Philomena—"

"Why did somebody attack Acie?"

"—she had a few things of his she didn't want underfoot, now that
he's passed—"

"Harnett, your dad. What happened to him?"

A sort of out-breath, almost a snort. "Long story, girl. I'll tell you
the all of it when I get a few things settled, but if you could help me out
with this, I know my aunt will be showing you her appreciation."

I didn't want to know. I asked, covered my other ear, his answer
streaming in anyway. "What do you have?"

"You know that artist, Beckmann?"

I stood with the telephone and moved to the window where, below,
Fifty-ninth Street streaked with car lights, and the dots of lit rooms
to the South Side blinked blankly in the night; beyond them, faint

trails, effluents of Gary, rose and were spirited northwest to Chicago. Four months in graduate school and I'd only a hustler and his father to show for it. It was time to apply myself to an end. Maybe one more beer tonight. Two beers, not bad—anyone would have two beers.

"Sorry, Harnett," I said. "Can't help you there."

But by morning I'd thought again.

"Bartel, could I bother you for a minute?"

He nodded, standing at his office bookcase tracing his thumb down a page, his head a good foot above mine. Because he stood, I stood, too, hovered at the doorway while his thumb moved from the book to the wisps of chin hair, almost a goatee.

"Did Beckmann do drawings?"

For a moment, Bartel, not seeming to hear, then his eyes drilling, then he turned to the shelf, back to me.

"Beckmann. Drawings." His curiosity more about me than my question, peering. "We always thought not many, there was no money in it for him. However. There *was* geld in drypoint during and just following the First World War, so—" He coughed, the cough racking him, I waited. "Close the door."

Stepping inside, closing the door so that Bartel could smoke. He crossed to the desk, lit a slender brown cigarette from a bright red pack, sat in his desk chair, and swiveled to look out the window at the roof below. Me, not much of a student, half a heart, skating through his Dada and *Die Brücke* and *de Stijl*, now suddenly tuned in and bothersome. "Smoke?" I shook my head, closed my eyes, felt my thirst. Knew a drink would right me.

Bartel had the shape of a Bartlett pear. "For a long time the primary evidence we had of his draftsmanship were his drypoints," he began. "Their immediacy seems to have appealed to him, and there are many examples only because they were so lucrative for him."

"Yes," everything quickening, "I've found reproductions of these."

He swiveled again, now regarding me, his eyes pricking my forehead and bearing in, as if inscribing, visually, the information on my brain.

"Since his death, drawings held privately until then have finally reached the market. Enlightening, these drawings." His thumb, perpendicular to the cigarette curled in his fingers, indicated the bookcase. "That's one."

Bartel had one! The German monograph had explained Beckmann's under-drawing of his paintings, beginning a canvas by sketching directly on the gesso, and then doing the graphic over-painting. The sketch on Bartel's shelf, small, small gilt frame, could have been one of those under-drawings but for its miniature size: two large eyes in Beckmann's familiar face, shadowed with cross-hatchings, under a dark cap at a strong tilt. A patterned curtain drawn over one shoulder and, at the base of the drawing, arms scarcely indicated but firmly crossed over the painter's chest. Straight from a self-portrait.

"Yes," Bartel said, as though in answer. "*Self-Portrait with Black Cap*, 1934. It's in Cologne."

"The painting?"

He nodded, smiled, *smirked*. "A year's mortgage, this study."

He waited while I studied it. "Has anyone reproduced his drawings anywhere?"

Bartel exhaled, stubbed the brown More on the rim of a ceramic urn, rose. "Scattershot. I have a Carus catalogue from '75. Somewhere." He rooted through a stack on a low shelf and pulled out a gray, square pamphlet. A price list inside the front cover—thirty-five hundred to twelve thousand a drawing—and an introduction. I opened, first pages—

Winter, 1945, pen and ink, no other information. A giant snowball in the picture's center, a snowman with billowing scarf behind it, a tall black teapot on a black stove (or elephant, or waving man?) in the doorway of a crude house on the left, an arrowed sign in front of a footbridge on the right. The center, the snowball, was a vacuum on the page. The idea that this might have passed through Acie's, like the other drawing, its being stuffed in brown paper, Acie's piss, making me queasy. But this drawing was clearly from Acie's painting. Or vice versa.

So they *were* Beckmanns in Acie's place.

"Miss Kinney." As I thanked him, leaving. Taking the stairs.

My boss in her fishbowl office, her "You were late," the rim of Hyde Park rising from the window behind her.

Yesterday I'd given Acie up. Given up Acie, Harnett, lure of music at night, the distraction of my afternoons in the nest of the store. There were certain canvases by Beckmann in which circus acrobats, half-dressed women, masked masqueraders, and musicians crowded one another and the corners of the canvases leaving no air, no room, no space for thinking or for striking out alone. So what if he had Beckmanns, so what if the worlds did, after all, intersect and *I* was the crossover, the guinea pig, the chump. I had my Good Orderly Direction to follow, my studies, a responsibility to myself, fears. I needed air.

And now, the slide library, no one else working, and my boss and her hot tea, settling in at the table's end beside me. There'd be bourbon before two. "So. What are you doing for Dr. Bartel's project?" Skeptical, thick-tongued, at my fever.

"Do we have slides of Beckmann's drawings?"

A long look. "So you have caught this bug from Bartel, too, huh?" But she rose, pulled a drawer, set it before me, and picked a slide at random, raising it warily to the light.

Of course, *Winter* was among them. Before me on the lightbox, it, a few black marks set off by the light, a typed label on the silver of the glass. The label gave the drawing's provenance as Dresden, far away, when the slide had been made, twelve years back. It gave its size— 85 x 90 cm, twice the size of Acie's painting. These were the details that sent me back to Record Palace, details that cast *iconography* and *style* in the frame of a cartoon, of a drawing, of a ticket to its mattering. On the way: a drink.

$\{$

The store reeked more than ever, Acie wearing a shirt I'd never seen him in—bright orange with two black stripes around a front placket, a few stains down the front, his raw scalp exposed, burnt-sienna of it heightened by the orange of the shirt. Not even looking at me, his friend Wyans giving him some papers and asking for a number, Acie piddling around with his piles while the dog Ma looked on. I flipped through the LPs in the bins up front, same old records. Same old.

What was his business? *Whom can I turn*—Stuffed it back, focusing on a Ramsey Lewis release. "Straight up six o'clock but straight," I heard him saying to Wyans who nodded to me, leaving.

Maybe I had been wrong, wrong about all of it. Why wouldn't his family have heirlooms?

"String bean supreme." He said it warily, slowly.

"What?"

"I said you are a string bean girl." No mistaking the edge.

Trying to look at his face, his taking the moment to bend and cluck to the dog. "Is your head better?" More growl than mumble in reply.

I'd come ready to forgive, to understand, and now it was me, *I* was the bad charm, repossession, mugging, scam. Acie undone by it.

"Say string bean, *what* is it you are studying in school?" Like a taunt.

I felt hurt well up, stuffed it back. It was dangerous, wanting attention, comfort, reassurance. "Art history—" The Beckmann, the painting of the fish in the monograph matching the drawing in Acie's bathroom, and the painting, the snowman, like the drawing in the slide: knowledge like a scrim on my focus. Maybe Acie hustled art, or something more monstrous, Harnett solider, saner—Acie's gun on him, a father, Harnett even present, the darkest—

"Acie. What happened the other day?" Looked at me, my voice like a train crash, a stammer full speed at a cow, "with the brick, with Harnett?"

"What?" Collapsed terrain of his face firming, enlarging. "You are the one to tell me."

I heard the click of the needle in an eccentric groove and Acie's wheezy breathing. That spinning sense. "What do you mean?" He glowered. "Acie, what did I do?"

His wandering eye on the wall, the other still on me. I waited. Minutes passed in his regard, fierce to fiercer, then a break.

"If you are going loco, girl, I want you to tell me. Now." Gruff, but beneath it an acre of tenderness.

The voice that only a moment ago I had thought I'd only imagined possible, just in order to damp my own despair, the voice that was Acie's and compassionate: the voice was the break in the sandbagging that triggered a flood now sweeping the streets.

I was inside the sobbing itself, I felt the jelly of Acie's body against my own and breathed in pure BO.

The el car has a sour smell, and the man takes a seat looking out across the door frame to the back of the next car, careful to face forward. The girl beside him has freckles, and when she takes off her gloves to loosen her scarf he sees her one hand has large blotched circles of brown skin on white. Everywhere, infirmity. It is God's cautioning and he is heeding.

He feels in his pocket for a matchbook. There are several, and he fishes them out in a clump on his palm until he is satisfied he has the one with the address scribbled on the striking side.

It is so quick he jumps. The man in the brown coat on the aisle has fallen to the floor of the car. The vibrations of the el seem to be wiring the man electronically, eyes careening back in their sockets. Trial one, he thinks, dropping to the floor, shoving his hand between the man's two sets of teeth, diving for a tongue. It is already flapped back like the rubber disc on a drain.

The el car seethes to a stop and hovers high

*above Argyle. There is a buzz. Then it is he hears
the duh DUH, duh DUH of "India's" opening bars.
duh DUH duh DUH, DUH DUH DUH duh DUH.
A cracker in an old jumpsuit swings a boom box
onto his seat, next to the freckled girl who seems to
be sleeping she is so nonplussed. Opened, "India"
wends off to its going out, the tangle of instruments
suddenly out there, chaotic and precise. He grips
the tongue, his haunch on the man's side, closes his
eyes, and listens hard.*

Acie

{

I am no sooner open after this long night of disturbance, my head raw with my scalped skin, than I see the cutouts *distributor*, name of Blue, pull up in the Skylark of his and honk his horn like he is the Queen of Sheba. The sun is out, too cold yet for slush, but I have no intention on taking the slap sandals out for a tour of the town green just to investigate the samples. When I ignore him, he locks up and looks around and comes to the door. He pokes his head in—the camel and his nose: he *knows* I won't be keeping him out—and says "Good morning, Mr. Stevenson."

Bowtie is cleared out and I have Ray Bryant picking the "Stick with It" blues bars on the ivories.

"Blue," I say.

He says "I've got some titles you may be interested in." Blue has been at this all year since he figured he could come out ahead by skipping the rent on his establishment and selling the samples out from the trunk of his Buick. All the proprietors of platters in Chi-town have been buying and selling the samples and so have I too, but Boss of

Bowtie and myself have been contemplating a boycott. Problem is it can bring in the green.

"Not unless you are supplying them here for my review."

He is a formal jiver and he pretends he does not see the scalp I have out to air itself. "What number are you in the market for today?"

"I am not *in* the market."

Door slams to behind him, but I know it is a bad sign, his being by first thing on a Monday.

I may have the gun on my person but I am still the maintenance man of this palace, and I got to clear some shit out. Cans, these trashy cups, got to get me a bag for this shit. Cigarette stubs on the floor, might as well be running an hourly here. We got Bowtie's funky shirt I am tempted to toss in the bag in addition. If I move the cutouts—

Staring at me are my brother's papers I had just begun to go through the other day. I could forget my johnson. Blue pokes all of himself through now.

"On this stool here?" He whistle-breathes and he drops the LPs on my perch.

"Go ahead," I say after the fact.

Because he is already skimming he uses a soft-sell technique which adds up to standing there with his mouth shut. I am not going to forget my brother's papers again and so I take my time securing them in an envelope and loading them into my waist. Blue thinks I am crazy so I can go a long way with making him wait before he squawks.

He has brought in sorry shit but the shit moves. It is a little late to be acquiring Art Pepper's "*Today*" but he has two copies in the pile plus Paquito d'Rivera that I know I can sell without blinking, "*In the Tradition,*" that platter Columbia is hot on by this Black Arthur Blythe, and the Milestone Jazz Stars that the youngbloods go for. Elvin's "*Remembrance.*" Blue may be a Joe Sad but he knows what I sell.

Door is up again. Wyans. I know from this I am jumpy, fuck this.

"Just one of the Pepper. The rest suits."

"That'll be eight," he says. Chicken feed may be but not to the chicken losing it. And my feathers are ruffled. Plucked.

Camel Blue looks like he wants to linger but a formal man needs an excuse. Wyans does not crowd but it is not necessary to crowd to be crowded in my moat. We hear louder than before the hi-hat Grady Tate playing on Bryant's version of the Duke's "C Jam Blues" until "Mr. Stevenson," Blue says, his hat getting a tip. The door bangs.

Wyans looks sharp but I can not figure it until my eye gets to his pants.

I have known him so long he can read my mind. "Natural fiber," he says. Despite this they do appear to be warm.

"So. Lay it on me."

"I had to spend a little, Ace."

Being reasonable I know money is the power of persuasion.

"Tune of ninety."

"Wyans—" Not even twelve hours into a week and I am out near a hundred. I could not afford my offspring under my care and I cannot afford him out from under. "You are behind the times anyway, I was at the Como Inn with the Philomena last night."

"Did she tell you where she's staying?"

"She is not at the Marva's place?"

"She's at the projects all right, Ace, she may be safest there." He eyeballs me like I am one sorry sack. "Projects seem to know your man for killing a child in tower three, five, six years back, daylight, no reason, the works. Dealers know him, so I expect he is a target over there."

"And the cat *be?*"

"No good." I would give Wyans my firstborn and should have long ago. He continues with the news. "The individual seems to have a lot of endeavors going, Ace. Not just the drugs. Remember Colty?" Man once filled Upchurch's guitar with the navy beans and another time chewing gummed Blakey's hi-hat one night at Roberts Show Club getting Billy Eckstine fumed. Did not succeed in getting this Colty the popularity as he had intended. "It's his brother, Ace, they've got about twelve years between them."

I weigh this. Colty had himself a screw loose. "Name of?"

"Brady. Brady Bonner." Colty and Brady sound like Eight Is Plenty. Knowing the Iguana is a Brady cuts him to size.

Wyans scratches himself, his nose, as I take in the information my offspring is in league with the lizard. What I did to deserve the loyalty of Wyans I do not know.

"Ace," and then he starts in careful with me, which steams me, "I did turn up something about William."

Careful with others is good but with me he misapplies it, especially in the case of my esteemed brother. "What? Make a mint off the medicine and embroil his nephew?"

"He did come into a lot of green, I heard, thirty years back, Ace, enough to buy out that contract he had at the Grand Terrace."

"Thirty years is old history." An Italian had imperialized the clubs and the liquor makers like several before him. Musicians worked off their contracts never out from under the obligation and buyouts were rare. Now the imperialists got a more subtle arsenal but disentanglement does not happen quicker.

Wyans may have a fault of persistence as his interrogation seems to include me. "You visited his house, right?"

"Philly's crib."

"Anything showy about the place?"

The papers in my pants scrape the jewels. "Papers I got says he was not even the owner of his name and you *know* the Philomena ate up all he had in sugar." I remove the papers and press the envelope with my palm.

"Did you visit?" He asks me again but I grunt and turn to the mess that is my second order of business. Whatever he is getting at better arrive soon. "Did he have pictures, paintings in the place?"

This stops me. "Why?"

"Word is he collected pictures." At my business this morning at the throne, the safekeeping package Philly left behind her opened up itself to two of Ma's doodles framed like they are the Mona Lisa.

The fine art. "Hah," I say. "Just my ma's. That is how he maintained himself in her good graces. He had admiration for her *out*put." Woman with the airs that she was she did this in an art *studio* to impress upon the bank employees of my father's the im*por*tance of *cul*ture.

"I don't know then." Wyans shakes his head and I resume collecting the refuse. "Did she ever make anything off of her hobby?" he asks.

How could she. Pictures the dog Ma could do with *its* output. I smile at this despite my own standing as sire of Lucifer himself.

"Let's see the papers you got," Wyans is saying to me. Wyans has been helped out of a jam with the ladies more than once by my ingenuity and he knows it. There are more reasons I got to trust him.

I am trying to remember anything showy at the Philly's but I draw a blank. Could tell him about the dish bin in the bathtub. Her dusting the roach motels. Fact was I could not shit without her disinfecting the throne. She got one of them date posters of William's from the Vanguard framed, and Ma's pictures, but there was nothing else that

I can recall. Wyans just stands by. I remove the papers from their envelope, crumpled.

He looks at one paper and then the next. He is tight with a cousin that is a lawyer. "These aren't going to tell you anything, Ace, they're the tax returns. Did he leave a will?"

Traffic spurts loud and then I hear the skip at the LP where Bryant has finished his piano playing. "I thought *they* are it." Wyans just looks at me. Both he and the dog Ma, dynamic duo.

"You file *your* returns, Ace?" Then he shakes his head and says, "That's another story, don't answer that." Intend not to. I put the Bryant aside and queue up *Neo Nistico*. Sal Nistico and Roy Haynes leaning into "Trouble."

"What you need concerning William is more information." Wyans scratches behind his head, looks at my head, and puts back on his hat. "Does his wife have the will?"

I snort thinking of the wife.

He looks a question at me and then he stacks the papers into the envelope. "Safety deposit box that you know of?"

"Philly is a dead end. Brick wall. Jail bars. We will not be getting through or in or past the Miss Philomena." The dog barks like she is trained to on the mention of evil spirits.

"A grieving widow will deny some consolation?" Wyans chuckles, and I get his drift, my man Wyans. Takes a friend to cozy to a truck like the Philomena. It is true that last night she was putty to the Washington. After he left she laid on me her Cabrini Club number, number that I had not contracted from her by other means. "You get this to Harold Washington," she said like I am running a match-making service in memorial to my dead brother. Wyans enjoys his large charge, grinning.

"I got her number I am supposed to pass on to Washington," but I am grinning, too.

"Harold? How's he?" Wyans says. Wyans is my man.

The girl comes down the steps and tips the door in. All we need is the return of the omen, and soon as she comes in Wyans folds his tent. He hands me back the papers like he is passing me a beverage and says, "You were getting that number for me, Ace."

Ronnie Mathews got a good piano going here, too, but it is Haynes that stands out among the sidemen like fireworks.

I can be the Barrymore, too. I find the napkin and copy Philly's phone number out for him. Wyans looks at the girl like she will be going straight to the enemy with the clue. "Straight up six o'clock but straight," I say not convinced of this myself but Wyans gets it, his eye drops. He even tips the cap when he leaves.

Do not mind me, just receiving the petitioners, me and the Pope got the same life. People come, people go.

Meanwhile I can not even get a piss like it would come out if I tried.

"Girl."

Why is it the ones that are always reading are the straight up six o'clock girls, you tell me. Scrawny and stringy, her stringy hair now in stringy loops. "You are a string bean."

"So?" she says. "How's your head?" Cagey.

She is a skin popper no doubt and the Bowtie has been supplying. I am nutted out, my head has not stopped hurting yet and no sleep.

"How's your head?"

"Talking," I say. It goes past her.

She says "Acie," and it dawns on me now that she is more high strung than the usual. I remind myself that some ways she is fixed on me and I may use this to my advantage.

Then I remember something. "What is it you are studying in school?"

"Art, Acie." She observes her self a polite pause but appears to be sitting on a hefty perturbation which does not take too long to erupt. "Acie, what happened with the brick?" More. "What happened with Harnett?" And then the girl gets at my hands. It takes me a moment to tell what she is *doing* with them, hand-*holding* now that is an idea thats time is come. So she is a little Ruth Buzzy in her string bean encasement. She got the cooch.

"What did you do with him?"

And I thought I was wigging. "Did I do with who?"

She drops it and she drops the hands and mumbles. It could be that she is in the dex or the detox. This the most balled up I have seen her ever, so I wait and the more I wait the more she squirms. Finally I say, "Something at you girl then I want to know about it."

This coming out of the blue stops her. I should have left her at it. Ninety bills, a will, a girl slopping the sobs, and still before two. "Girl," I say. And before I know it I have myself a bale of straw in my arms like the old days. But this one shakes like it is the first time for her. Crying, that is.

I get her off me without a stiff one, which is not much of a feat these days. I have her watch the front while I try to urinate thinking she will compose herself, but staring into that dark water does not seem to do it so I pull it all down and sit on the throne and wait, the skin on my head hurting full a headache and dizzy making. I should have given her the alarm on. I know I need to piss. I should get back to the front. Bowtie is in a heap of, Philomena in a heap of, I in a heap of, now the girl not even my relation—That slobbering would have gotten to Lazarus before his rise-up.

I do the checklist. Icebox door shut. Sink water on. Still nothing. Light hazy in here by the bulb in the room but motion catches my eye and the animal is gone in the wall. I pick up the package and open the paper again and regard the fine art. Up front, she puts some crazy piano on I do not recognize and if she has been at the inventory re-moving the wraps she can boohoo to Christmas for the good it will do for her. Fine art. Now we got a stuttering tenor and I know which one she has, where the Spanish cat tries to out-Sonny the Dollar Brand. Here go the screeches.

Cannot seem to get the drift of Ma's doodles. A giant fish is what I see. She turns up the section where Top Dollar repeating the bass on one hand playing tambourine with the other, and Gato the Cat trying to wrench a gut with the dramatics.

Girl, you just stay away from here awhile. Whatever happens to me does not involve you. Go read your books.

She could assist in my investigation, if she is not assisting the other side.

What am I a gumshoe? And where are her people.

A trickle creeps out. Then I know somebody has come in with her talking out front and the urge is there but no more leisure for compliance. The Incredible Hulk tries to bring in the white guy with a chin in *The Lonely Are the Brave* but his helicopter crashes, and it is Archie Bunker himself and his truckload of toilets that hits the cowboy and his horse in the dark. Incredible Iguana is on my tail now, but I know it will be the plumbing that does me in.

The pants come up, wet, hell. Girl, you *got* a ma somewhere so you get yourself to *her*.

Funny how the suitors rush in when you need to voyage to the throne. In my palace there is now a full house. Fearless Freddy the One-Stop Wonder channeling the charm at the girl by the door and, at the bins, the Shadow I Know. The cadaver palaver, stinger with a zinger. Fan of the Cab Jivers. Iguana with the ikebana.

I get the girl to leave. When I see her on the pay phone in the Hop Sing window I think I should be in line for the Mensa. Wyans off at the Philly's crash pad will get what is up. Meanwhile the Iguana prattles at me.

"Brotherman."

"It is beyond my abilities to reconstitute the Cab Jivers," I say, knowing the Cab Jivers were not ever what he had on his mind. What he does have involves the spring-off of my loins.

"I no longer need the Cab Jivers. I am in need of the cash. The bill due is twelve and rising." He lights himself a death tube and takes a good suck in. "You can pass along to your relations their final notice or you can pay up on their behalf." Dog Ma has got the low growl on her.

Getting it on with Bowtie's ma is my best memory. Still don't make up for the sorry-ass result. And if the offspring will not inform me, I will insure his creditor does. "What services are you billing?"

"Brotherman, I understand you were summa cum laude," rasp of the Iguana, "so you don't have to be playing the ignoramus." The eyebrow he raises makes an ensemble with his curled lip.

"You have mistaken me for my dead brother. Of whose *business* I and my relations have no knowledge. So unless you eradicate the jive and shoot straight I am happy to serve you outright what you have been serving myself."

But I do not get myself the chance to fulfill the promise. The door opens on a customer name of Washington.

The woman in the low-cut beige sheath leans across the table toward his wife. She has pushed the salad plate into her name card, so that he can't make out who she is; behind her, the Tyrannosaurus in the Hall of Dinosaurs glowers in the candlelight. Benefits. "Marilyn," the woman's urgent voice is saying, and then a laugh. What is it, these women and Marilyn Monroe? Some kind of fad. He's had to bid on the signed photograph, as though coming to an event in this musty museum isn't torment enough. His wife's eyes are bright above the floral extravaganza in the center of the tablecloth, and when he catches them for a moment she blushes like a girl.

A long introduction by the Field Museum's chief curator finishes behind him, and applause ricochets in the cavernous hall. A scientist with a boyish air named Stephen Jay Gould taps at the microphone he's mounted, shrugs a thank you to his apologist, and says he has come to describe the panda.

Cindy

It was probably coincidence, the slight old man and the salesman coming in at the same time. I'd embarrassed Acie into extricating himself with "watch the front," embarrassed myself, still dizzy, looking for a nip behind the kibbles. Just get yourself right. A little sip would help.

The salesman smiling smarmily, speaking right up, the old fellow looking around with sharp, weary eyes, pulling from a bin the same Ramsey Lewis I fingered what seemed like hours ago.

"I'm here for Acie," the young one said, swinging a black case onto Acie's stool. A bassoon, a gun case, automatic weapons beneath these latches, his smile from ear to ear. "He around?" He was tall and skinny, *familiar, too,* with a taller-than-usual kufi of blue embroidered silk.

"He'll be right out." It sounded tentative and I knew I should be firm. Get yourself together.

I was a whirr, a whirl. Everything double-time, speeding, hightailing.

"You work for Acie?" He, talking quickly, the words skimming me. "I'm Hakim Redding, representing Warner, Elektra, RCA Victor. Here's my card." I bought time, putting the Gato Barbieri and Abdullah Ibrahim duet, "Confluence," onto the turntable, lowering the needle, and when the music started he raised his voice. Watching us over a Ramsey Lewis jacket, the old man.

"He'll be right out." Firmer this time. Gluing. Good.

Acie's flip-flops slapped in the aisle behind me.

"Freddy I am short too much this morning as it is."

"How's it going, Acie? Did you listen to the Jackie McLean slick?"

"I can be less polite about it, Fearless, if you need me to." Calmed me, the voice alone, calmed me down. But he, the gun, forgeries—

A squall of irritation knotted the rep's face, then released to more blue sky and smarm. "*You* tell *me*, Acie—just trying to serve your inventory needs. When do you want me to come by *again?*" Rep winked at me, big mistake, fella, if you think the one eye doesn't see patronizing for what it is.

Wedged into the gate aisle between Acie and his stool where the rep stood buckling up the black case in front of him. I was with Acie, *management*, more than I was with customers, the old man or salesman, Acie trusting me with the gate and now he was black. I meant, back. The rep out the door.

Sudden headache, clamping my forehead, drilling. Flap on my shoulder bag, unzipping the top, searching the mess for aspirin, Kitzinger on the middle ages, old Biba eyeshadow, cough drops free of their box and sticky. The door slamming after the rep, getting the aspirin and now for a drink, letting my bag go, Acie's face fuming and fixed on the old man.

Knowing I could leave buzzed around me like a fly. Ignoring it, waving it away. I would *help.*

"Acie, I need to check something." He didn't look at me, and I maneuvered past him into the maze of back bins, he scowling, taking the needle from the LP I'd put on. The mirrors were still up in the corners but no laser light in them, the cement walls under the bulbs marked with splotches and wear, the crates serving as bins sagging at their sides. The quiet made me reluctant to look at either Acie or the man.

"Girl I need somebody to do my shopping again. You take this list?" I looked up. Acie was holding a cocktail napkin and a bill between his first two fingers, his eye fixed on the old man.

No music, my buttons brushing against the bins making a clatter like a snare-drum break, my buttons, Acie holding the napkin out, sucking in his breadth as I passed. The sun had burned through the overcast of the morning, and there was sunlight through the stairwell window, casting a wedge on the old man's shoulder as I looked back at him from the door. So where was Harnett now?

The year David painted his death of Marat, Eli Whitney invented the cotton gin. I memorized this by thinking of the machine's hopper as Marat's long arm careening down the painting, Marat dead in his turban, letter and quill in hand, the green felt of his writing board meeting the blood in his bath only on the canvas. Only in paint.

In daylight, on the napkin, in a curved, neat hand, a name, "Philomena Stevenson," and a number, "397-4552," stood out in blue ballpoint ink. The "i" of "Philomena" was dotted with a heart. What the fuck—

Such a girl! Little dizziness, few tears, and I was back in it. A chump. Leda, readying herself for the swan. At least with the real mom I could name the enemy and pour it, join it. But now back in league with Acie, art appraiser, and his forger son.

Hop Sing's across the street had a pay phone, blare of the kitchen radio. *And now, top of the charts one year ago and still one of our most-requested songs. Re-u-nited. By the ever-loving Peaches and Herb.*

When the quarter clinked into the telephone box it stayed there, no beat in the dial tone registering it, the change lever not bringing it down. Dialed anyway.

"Please deposit twenty-five cents for three minutes." Through Hop Sing's picture windows, the hotel and Record Palace's stairwell. Two dimes. Three. So Acie had a wife. A drunk hesitated, hauled himself up onto the ice of the hotel's top step, right under a line of icicles. Maybe I should have gotten a beer first.

"Hello?" A wife.

Why was I calling? "Hello, is this Philomena Stevenson?"

"Who is this?" The drunk leaned back on the steps.

"This is Cindy Kinney. I'm a friend of Acie's."

"Hold on, honey." I heard muffled speaking; voices were raised behind the loud garble of a hand on a receiver. Then another voice.

I'd get the clerk's attention for a beer. Oblivious. A Hop Sing delivery man along the window, shading his eyes with a takeout menu, let the door bang its overhead bells, raising the window counter, disappearing into the kitchen behind. The muffled voices stopped.

"This is Mrs. Stevenson speaking." Acie, a wife.

"Mrs. Stevenson, this is Cindy Kinney. Acie just asked me to call you."

"*Yes?*" Waiting for her to fill me in until it dawned then, she's waiting on *me*. "And what does Acie Stevenson *want?*" Hostility in her voice. So, divorced.

"I don't know, actually. He gave me the number a few minutes ago—there was someone else in the store and I got the feeling—"

"Mr. Stevenson did not give you a clue?"

"Sorry. I'd hoped you'd know."

Muffled voices again, then knocking. "I wish I did, young lady." A man's voice, now, in the background. "We have us a visitor here, but you tell Mr. Stevenson we are all just fine."

{

I was seven, we left the Valley and drove farther inland, a car trip, a day trip, like other families, my father still there, the sun hot on the lid of our Buick, 7-Up in their cooler for me, cold, as cold as I would want it, and dripping as it came out of the lazy ice. Left alone in the backseat to color Hoss standing by the dry well, thinking maybe my mother's door would accidentally open and she would fall out and be squashed by a truck but not dead yet so we would have to "put her to sleep," my father and me. Our neighbor Julian had had to put his dog to sleep and it was irreversible. The windows down, now fields, now sprinklers like upended grasshoppers twenty miles high, I don't care if I do exaggerate, I saw them. There was a book on the pocked green seat, I could read most of it, one of those fuzzy books, the chicks in their mangey, yellow mold and the dog gummy from licking, where I had taken Julian's head and pushed it onto the page and wouldn't let go until he licked it all over.

My father turning us onto a dirt lot in front of a fall-down kind of building with a big sign: *Coyote Ranch*, drawings of dogs on it. I want to bring my 7-Up with, my mother saying, *no, we're leaving our drinks, you have to leave yours,* near my face so that the smoke coming from her mouth gets in my eyes, and when the smoke clears behind her and behind the shack there is a fence and a few lazy dogs lying out under the sun, not even getting up as my father walks over, a fat man coming out now from the hut kind of place and walking toward my father. I acquiesce with the pop, I'm shirking out of my mother's reach, I'll be there before she gets there, and the man and I reach my father at the same moment. The dogs are all a kind of flesh color, just blobs in the ratty grass, one of them is lying flat-out with bubbles coming out of his mouth, grrrrring. "Yeah, I have to put that one to sleep, but not in front of the little one," the man is saying to my father. How did he read my mind? But there she is, my mother. My mother walks over to the building and drops her cigarette in the dirt outside before she goes in, weaving almost so no one else would notice at the door. Bubbles happening anywhere, anytime, to anyone.

Or icicles. From where I sat at Hop Sing's window counter I could see the other side of the street for three blocks. Acie's window was a black hole in the blaze of the sun on snow. Five minutes ago a man had come out of the hotel in his shirtsleeves and shoved the drunk aside with his foot, the drunk still a C on the stoop, passed out on the salted ice below the dripping icicles. Hop Sing's radio unfurled the last of *again, naturally.* Fade-out. *Gilbert O'Sullivan, number one on the golden hit parade for sixteen weeks in 1972.*

Deciding what to do, another beer. I could walk away, walk away,

I could try to find Harnett, put him on the spot, find out what's after Acie, I could walk away. Another opportunity to fucking waffle. If I weren't white, would it have been easy? *No.* I'd have said *no.* Bullshit, the assumptions I made. Open my throat to this gold. The gold of the coyotes. Coyote pups.

Leon Golub swimming to mind, *his* drawings, this head of mine. He was my age when he did drawings of heads, drawn ferociously, quickly, with sometimes only a hasty scrawl to indicate an eye, a furrow, the electricity of thinking. One drawing crammed three heads, like herms, one toppled before the others, their Picassoesque prim features countered with smudged patches of fervent scribbling, borders. *Monolithic Conversation Piece.* I didn't know why this had come to me, except for the dog, for the dog in this drawing. I needed fewer heads.

Two-forty.

Chinese Bronzes would just be over. Professor Landow would bow slightly at the close of each class, as the lights came up and the projector's beam was turned off, fan still running, another student critiquing the lecture from the slide booth, the professor gone, the rest of us milling. I'll bolt Acie's. It's all just fear that keeps me.

So. Greater in being alone, this fear, than in a *noir* scenario with a one-eyed man.

A deep red Cadillac Seville glided to the curb across the street. "—luego," the man at Hop Sing's said, hanging up the phone at the takeout counter. Two men got out of the Seville, disappeared down the stairwell to Record Palace.

"Another, lady?"

Sudden resolve, dumping the bottle in the bin, rousing. "No, couple coffees, light, to go," and I paid with Acie's twenty.

A driver idled the Cadillac on the street before Record Palace. I could still walk away. Acie's door opened into a man, a wall of one, "—Brady Bonner," he was saying and then, seeing me, "Oh, please excuse me, Acie, I'm getting in the way of all your business," as he turned and stepped aside at the same time. Peppery head of hair, eyebrows thick above a bemused expression, an expensive cut to his overcoat and suit. Amused by me, at Acie's? His hat in his hands.

The old man was still there, up front, too, nothing was said while they made room for me at the front bins. What did Acie have going?

If we were going to play spy, I'd pretend I was a casual customer, set the coffees on the concrete floor. The old man was leaning on the front wall, and the bins—had I memorized the LPs in this one yet?—were mine. The old man took in the coffees, took in me, I stared back at him until he feinted. My father, punching me—learning to punch him back.

"Acie, I sure could use that Milt Hinton down at campaign head-quarters. Do you have it in stock?" Out of a whole other film, a comedy, a domestic comedy, the woolly man's voice. He made a motion to defer to me should I have needed something but I waved no, feeling the old man's presence, his gaze. "And it troubles me to trouble you, Acie, but if you have facilities I might use, you could feel free to increase your retail prices."

"You find the new Milt Hinton, girl, and I will show this congressman-to-be the throne," Acie said, nodding to him without taking his eye from the old man. Congressman. Turning, following Acie, both behemoths in the aisle. My cover blown, I picking up the coffees from the floor, standing again, the congressman almost to Acie's beaded curtain when the old man spoke.

I was there by some mistake, blown in by chance before the full gale hit and I'd be buried under the rubble and the records. He was speaking to me, I was no longer invisible to everyone but Acie, being now a part of whatever had happened, was happening, would happen. I thought of Bobbi and for a moment I panicked. Wait, this is not the scene I'd hoped for. "'Day," he said, moved toward the door, my breath held; and then the congressman stopped, turned, planted himself in the back of the store. Still smiling.

A charge lit the still air like a lightning strike along a telephone wire. I thought of Acie's gun, of all I didn't know. *Drop,* telling myself, but I couldn't move, watching the old man reach for the door.

"Brady Bonner." Acie's politician, his resonant voice. The old man stopped, his hand on the door handle, his back to the store, not turning, his head down. I wanted him gone, the old man odorous of menace, I wanted the politician to say, "No, go on," the store would return to being mine, mine and Acie's and the usual men—knowing, though, that it wouldn't, I'd touched him, cried on him, and Acie had held a gun on his son.

"Before you depart, I am bound to tell you," and the congressman paused, "I do have a special interest in Mrs. Taylor, mother of that Cabrini boy who got himself shot out of nowhere in 1973, and knowing that she has on hand a full five witnesses to that unfortunate event gives me a certain responsibility to alert her to your presence again in our *boun*tiful city." The man drawled it, taking his time, still amused, he blocking Acie's face but I could see Acie's arms hanging at his side. That the man at the door, the old man, killed someone, and a child, I could believe. *Breathe.* But what did it have to do with Acie? "Besides, you may know, Brady Bonner, I am running for office now and if I brought a killer in for justice it would win me a lot of favor." What did it have to do, at last, with me?

"You may also know that when I had my chance I spent my own time in Cook County. I got to know quite a few long-timers who owe me a favor or two, so I am in the fortunate position of assisting in your discomfort wherever you end up."

Cook County, the jail. This man running for congress was in jail?

"Unfortunately, Brady, I do have something of a profile. If that does not deter your animosity, you may be interested in the fact that I am not here alone. So there would not be much of a chance of your leaving my friend Mr. Stevenson's with your earthly form intact."

Acie and his friend, in the back of the store, consulting, the old man turning the doorknob. What was I doing here? Icy air cutting into the store.

"One more advisement, Brady." Cold slicing. "Leave Mr. Stevenson and his family alone. We have a city-wide organization and we can find you before you can say Oliver. If I *ever* hear you are at them again, your sleeping nights are over. Go on." Irritation supplanting humor on the speaker's face, bang of the door behind me. The old man was gone.

"You getting the Hinton?"

"Toilet, Acie," the man said, smiling again, two of them disappearing behind the curtain.

Beckmanns by the toilet. A "congressman." I, missing a code, a meta-language, a ticket. I remember the dankness in the store that day, the cold, the confusion. Knowing it had nothing to do with me. Right yourself. Leave. Let him get his own Hinton. But some threat, it seemed, had passed.

Milt Hinton. Didn't know if I'd ever heard a Milt Hinton record, unless here and I didn't know it, more of that middle-age man's music Acie touted. One's cover looking like it was done by Alfred Jensen, numbers sprawling in blue and red over a black and white checkerboard. The bin was full, I started to look for recording dates when Acie came back through the beads, curtain clattering. He shuffling forward in his flip-flops as if he was elderly and infirm.

It seemed awkward, suddenly, being there.

"I got you some coffee," I said, holding one of the cups out to him.

"Did you call that number?" He took the cup and set it down again.

"Acie, is that your wife?"

He looked at me as though I was nuts.

"This number," passing him the napkin, "this woman."

He turned away, mumbling, not really to me. "Wyans not there yet, no Wyans—" Acie peeled the plastic top off the cup. "You take your coffee dressed up?" He turned back then, looking straight at me. "Because I do not."

"Sorry—" but he waved me off.

"A mixed thing, assistance."

He was putting Don Byas on the turntable. Byas's legato—an old LP, mid-fifties—setting up Mary Lou Williams's piano, just behind the beat, restrained without being delicate, just a quick on-off with the notes, with her using the pedals to clip the notes in place. Music seeming to relax the very air.

Focusing on it brought my heartbeats in line.

"Find the new one?"

I held up *The Trio*.

"No, that one is not a new one." So easy it would have been for him just to come around the aisle and pull it himself. "You know Milt Hinton is a photographer as well as a bass player."

"Do you remember, Acie, Milt telling us how Eddie South was impelled to stand behind a screen to accompany Bea Palmer at the

College Inn?" The curtain swaying, clattering behind him as the congressman came down the aisle, behind him the toilet repeating, acting up. "It was not that long ago."

He looked at me; I felt myself blush under his attention. "The College Inn would not have a black musician accompanying a white woman."

They both: standing, quiet, listening. Above the plumbing, the piano picked out an Oriental scale, swung back into the unfamiliar ballad where Byas caught it and stretched the final note, flattening it slightly. Surreal it was, the man's threats still in my ears, all of the goings-on just moments ago, and Acie and he acting now like nothing had happened. I'd go.

Sudden crack, I turned, the door opened—on Wyans, squinting, animating when he saw the man in the aisle. "The bear with the hair!" he said. "Ace was saying he saw you around."

I was a third—fourth—wheel, an extra, trying to focus on what returning to my room would feel like, what the library and tomorrow's Bartel class would feel like. My room, small, bright, vacant, bare, vacant, a quarter of a gallon of Jim Beam's left. The third wheel, the extra, I'd be in the seminar, or in the library, watching other students whisper together, laugh.

Wyans and the candidate shook hands, leaning into each other as though they would hug but they didn't.

"Mr. Albert Wyans. Long time."

"Has been, Harold, but I've been following your endeavors."

"Hope that means a vote, Wyans. Now, where's that platter?" The man's smile was a million-dollar smile, a beacon on a dark night, safety. I'll register; *I'll* vote. But now, when Wyans moves over, I'll follow the congressman out. I'll go.

"My assistant is still in training," Acie, scowling, picking an album off the top of the stack beside him and turning it over to the candidate. "You need a bag?" An album that wasn't in the Hinton bin.

"What do I owe you, Acie?" Byas dipping into a faster tempo.

Acie didn't look at the man, flapped one elbow away from his side, his hands already full of papers. "Go on."

"Now, I can't be taking payoffs from the constituents—"

"The hides you just sa—" Acie began.

Washington waved his arm. "I don't want to know, Acie. What's private for you is none of my business." He put on his hat, I saw then that he was my height, no more, just big. "Obliged to you. Albert, Acie, Miss." Ducking as he went through the door frame, although his hat was a good foot under it.

That was my cue.

In my first art history class ever, as an undergraduate, my professor gave us Wolfflin to read on the linear and the painterly and then spent six weeks on the notion of the picturesque and the sublime. The picturesque, he maintained, was busy, fussy, focused on scenes of domestic sentimentality and on ruins that provoked the banal feelings of nostalgia. The sublime, according to Edmund Burke, was a fear and then delight that would overtake us in the presence of something mighty, mammoth. It struck our greater sensibilities, in its severity elicited the part of us we fix on god, and transported us—or wrenched us—from our more earthbound preoccupations.

At least this is how I remember it. By the time I got to graduate school I had learned about the Kantian sublime, too. But I had also learned that the idea was filed away behind the Barthes and the Derrida. Rembrandt's self-portraits, paintings my professor cited as paradigmatic, were heavily coded representations of our *ideas* of the sublime, as constructed and as artificial as Zsa Zsa's hair.

"I hate these meal coupons, they're all over my purse!"

The girl, hearing this as she embarked on her chef's salad in Hutchinson's Commons, was thin, and as she was not too rich she was, maybe, too thin. Gaunt. She hadn't bothered to take the knitted hat from her hair, and her scalpline was damp, her nose and cheeks still red.

The girl with the purse settled her things on the chair beside her. "Anyway, sorry, go on." She removed the plates from her tray.

"No, neither, really. My father left ten years ago, so I have no idea what he's doing now. And Ma's on disability but it's just a hobby to support her drinking career." A drop formed at the base of her nose and, embarrassed, she made a pass with her napkin.

The other girl kindly looked away. "Oh, I'm sorry." Her sympathy was palpable, and the girl in the hat appeared to be surprised at this.

"Oh, there's Benjamin! Benjamin!" the other girl called and watched as the man turned around, waved, neared. "He's a sweetheart."

Harnett

The times when my uncle paid a visit from New York to my grand-mother he brought me playing cards. Every deck had a different picture: the Statue of Liberty, a plate heaped with ribs, Dinah Shore, a geisha woman with a spread fan, and at night he taught me how to play. He had broad shoulders, slick clothes, and he smelled like a man should, not embarrassing like the musk of my father or the witch hazel of my grandfather.

When I was in middle school my uncle brought me the records he'd just pressed, and answered when I asked him who he'd played with lately and what other musicians thought of my mom. As on every visit he took Ivie out "for coffee," but by then I understood. I *did* want to be him—and not just for that.

He and Aunt Philly took with them always a stack of my grand-mother's paintings and drawings, wrapped in white paper from the big roll my grandfather brought home from the butcher.

"What do you do with her paintings?" I asked. William didn't answer, but my grandfather said, "Your grandmother's art has distin-guished collectors."

{

By the time my grandmother died, her beef with my uncle William was not only over his hooking up with Philly, a white woman, but over my grandmother's paintings. Opportunities to put my talents to use hadn't yet presented themselves, and I was so messed up I wanted to get on something harder and stay on it. "There's a ticket waiting for you at O'Hare," Aunt Philly said. "Two o'clock American flight to LaGuardia. We'll meet your plane."

I called my boss at the Bebop Shop and paid a cab to O'Hare. It was mid-afternoon, and the driver was tuned in to Hardly a Dick. My uncle's "Once a Rainbow" was the intro on the half-hour, and the windows on the cab were down in the heat, so I asked the driver to raise the volume, turn it up over the rush of the air and cars on the expressway. The swing in Dannie Richmond's drums swelled. We spouted music like steam from a steampipe, the steam overtook the cars around us, and a man in an Oldsmobile shot me the peace sign as he passed.

Ivie's was a hot, vacant space over a supermarket on Avenue C. I leaned on a wall and watched my aunt sop her cleavage; the Kleenex left white burls on her tits.

"Ivie has your grandmother's business to run. But it doesn't make any sense for her to stay in Chicago when we can look after her here." My uncle nodded at what Philly said, but he wasn't watching her sop like I was. "We thought it was time you came out and saw us, we know how much you loved your grandmother, we hope you'll help Ivie pack up and keep things smooth with your dad now."

"This is bigger than Grandma's studio," was all I could think to say.

My aunt replied, "Now Ivie can have her own assistants. Your grandmother schooled her like a daughter and she's ready to fly."

I packed up Ivie and the studio. My father watched me go off to do it, but he kept any reservations to himself. Ivie had always been retiring, but as I packed and then as I unpacked her in New York, her directions were strident and forceful, as though some of my grandmother's spirit had entered her, when she passed. I hadn't ever stopped wanting her, but my allegiance to my uncle overcame temptation.

"Your grandmother was an extraordinary artist," she said, sitting across from me at the kitchen table, still in its padded bumpers from the move. "You know she had a lifelong correspondence with a famous European artist." With her left hand, she raised her glass of iced tea and closed her eyes. "She wrote to him after she saw an exhibition of his paintings way back when and he wrote her back, and then she met him once, when he moved to St. Louis."

"What artist?"

Ivie had stood and now she bent over a box of paints and jars. "Harnett, let's get to this box before your uncle comes." And then she said, apropos of nothing, "Nice to be out of Chicago."

I asked my father if I could have my grandmother's house. "You paying the tax?" he said, and then he sold it through Bella Drake, the realtor, to a white family I wouldn't think to visit. When the money came, I deposited it for him and stood in line for the two cashier's checks: one to Uncle William and one to my mom, less my own small charge for the handling. I left the bank—it was an early day in spring and there were still patches of dirty snow—climbed into the car and lit a joint. Inhaling, it tasted like shit, literally, like manure wrapped in paper and inflaming my mouth with its sulfur, its coliform. I put it out and rolled another, same thing. I stopped by Linton's and tried different merchandise, a whole different genre, something not from Colombia this time but from Guyana. I watched him screen its seeds in front of me, I saw that it was vegetal, not dark, not digested, not shit, but when I lit up my sample it filled my lungs with the reek of feces. "Try oregano," said Linton, laughing. I was his best broker before we fell out.

I went to New York for a long weekend for Linton and stayed with Ivie, who had room for me, and visited my aunt and uncle, who did not. Aunt Philly threw down the keys in a glove wet from an August thunderstorm. She had various manicure tools and bottles lined up on the table in front of her, among ashtrays and dishes made into ashtrays and a bottle of Old Grand-Dad, and the phone was ringing as I opened the door.

My uncle came out of the bedroom where the TV was on and greeted me. Then he started to poke around, opening cabinets, looking for something.

The gasping sound Aunt Philly made on the phone stopped him cold. "Hold on. Let me get Will," she said, and handed him the receiver. She wore rings on every finger except her thumbs, and with all of them beside her face she looked paler than usual.

My uncle listened, and I listened to him listening; he hung the receiver back on the wall phone, his large hand quaking at his side. I hated seeing him distressed. "What happened?" I asked. Aunt Philly shot my uncle a look before she answered.

"You remember Bud Depries?" I remembered talk always at my grandmother's house about an Oscar Depries. "Well, Buddy was his cousin. He just had himself a heart attack and passed on."

"You were tight?"

My uncle stirred behind Philly. "Going to have to find another dealer, that's all." He seemed to overlook our being there. I had wondered but never known if my uncle used. Dealers were something I could help with.

"I can get you what you need."

For a moment I thought my aunt would slap me. My uncle closed the bedroom door behind him.

"It's not that kind of dealer, honey."

The next day Aunt Philly had emptied the ashtrays. William sat at the kitchen table running scales on his bass and looking at me while he did it. It wasn't something you could really converse over.

"Harnett, honey, you're an enterprising young man. Do you know anything about Ivie's art?"

My uncle stopped finally, still looking at me. The kitchen seemed bare without the woody sound reverberating in it.

"We wanted to ask you about something. We need you to keep it confidential by your dad, he don't need to know." When she said this, William lay his bass back in its open case and latched the lid. Then he lit a cigarette off of Philly's.

"Bud Depries went off to school." As Philly talked, William exhaled the smoke through both his mouth and his nose. "Yale it was, only the finest. Got a first degree, then went on for a second and then a third—he was the model for your grandmother of an achiever to be proud of. He came back to Chicago and worked a bit for a art dealer and then finally he opened a business of his own. Not a gallery per se, he didn't want to be tied down to any bricks and mortar, but he had the connections, he could sell on the side, he heard about your grandmother's painting and came to see it and then he couldn't make enough of it until your grandmother had agreed to sell her paintings through him. Your uncle William arranged it on account Bud was his best friend.

"Your grandmother copied what she liked. All the artists do that, honey." William put his cigarette on the floor, and ground it with his shoe, then lifted the butt to the dish. "Sometimes Bud Depries brought in even more for those copies than for her other paintings, her more *original* work. This was a fact she never knew."

My uncle crossed to the sink and looked out the window as though he wasn't listening to Aunt Philly. At the refrigerator he pulled out a packet of bologna and carried it with him back to the window, leaning against the sink, plying the circles out of the pack and rolling them. He was still the man I wanted to be.

"Bud took on Ivie when your grandmother passed and she was learned fine by your grandma and also she has had, with Buddy's help, her finger on the market. So now we have to find us somebody new to sell what Ivie paints."

I didn't have three degrees but I'd been to Circle and I had one. And I could sell anything. Hadn't I found takers for the packs of Ban Lons that Rakim came into once? And not just the low-end shit. The Pierrot chef-man, the one I had hooked up for the tropical flowers, I knew he would go for some art. I would bowl my uncle over. This was my ticket to suc*cess.*

"Let me do it."

"Oh honey," my aunt said. "We need someone who knows the world of art."

"I do, I know painting, I took art, I have an *aesthetic.* In Chicago— I've got contacts, high rollers. I swear to you." I hard-sold it like I never would have another transaction, knowing to hang back closed a deal. My aunt looked like she regretted she'd told me.

"Give me a go. Let me try it with one, with a couple—see how fast I can turn them over, and I'll prove it to you. Let me try."

My uncle had said nothing from where he stood at the window, but now he began to lay it out. "You'd be selling fakes. Got it? Not the up and up. So we need them handled in a careful manner. You can't be calling attention to yourself."

He didn't look at me, crossed to the table and lit another cigarette, inhaled, and sat down backwards in the chair. Big but lithe like bass players can be. "We need you to keep this completely confidential. Can't be telling your father." He looked at me. "The money is good." He smiled.

I wanted to look at the table but my eyes locked on Aunt Philly's pointy tits and wouldn't unlock. There were things, *goods,* I could get. New car, AR turntable, a leather coat.

My aunt looked gloomily at William.

"This is how it works." My uncle twirled the ashes tip of his cigarette on a jar lid until it came to a point. "We send you the pieces, you keep your own record, you keep 25 percent. Then you give a quarter to a fellow downwind of the business, to keep it on the QT, fellow who keeps it on the QT in Chicago and New York. Brady Bonner. You send the rest to us and we give it to Ivie and the overhead. Simple as pie but it requires finessing."

The TV droned in the bedroom. "You won't be sorry," I said.

"Well, Harnett dear, you have the enterprising spirit for it," my aunt said to me, sighing, and opening the Old Grand-Dad with a click. "You always have been so enterprising and independent." She poured an inch in an old cup and offered it to me.

"We'll start you with two."

{

"So, my grandmother's paintings were fakes?" I asked Ivie.

"She did some copies, honey, but she never knew how Depries was selling them as." She stretched out her long fingers and yawned. Her high cheekbones matched any woman's I could think of. "My own I know and they have brought in good money, better all the time."

I sold the two paintings by the middle of September to the chef, and when I told my uncle for how much, my uncle whistled in his breath. I paid off Brady Bonner. Then the chef bought two more paintings and I sold a drawing to a countess who comes into the Bebop Shop.

And then the market for the product slowed up.

"The clients are just getting the financing together, Philly, any day now," but every day it dragged me down a little further. Lying to my uncle wasn't the same as lying to Acie, or to The Hymen. And then this girl was on the scene, this art major, she knew art collectors, we would be partners, her and me, her contacts and my own gift at sales. I was just building up trust.

Come November, Philly called every day, and Brady Bonner began to call me, too. "Someone on your end is holding out," he said. I said no, just a slowdown in sales, but when my uncle died he upped the ante. When Philly called me in the middle of the night to tell me about William, I'd already spoken to each of them once, hours before. Then it was my father on the phone with a crack in his voice. "The funeral," he said, "is not for budhead nephews."

The receptionist in the pale green pantsuit opens the door of the inner office and waves the two women inside. A single line of photographs circles the green room, and the small man behind the rosewood desk rises, smiles with one brow cocked, and holds his spread hand out to indicate their seats. The women sit, adjust the brims of their hats, and smile, fetchingly.

"So you ladies want a liquor license to re-open the Bar None," he says. He folds his hands on the desk in front of him and looks from one large face to the other.

"We were told you could help us," the one with the decolletage begins.

"Sure I can. I do have a policy for the ladies, however. Our jobs here are jobs fit for Job, we work the long hours; it is a rare event when we are able to take a night off, and so you see my service to the city has made me a lonely man. If you ladies can find it in your hearts to give my soul some balm, you will find your license in your hand."

Cindy

When the door fell to, Acie looked at his friend Wyans for a long moment. His orange scalp glowed, his eyes were ringed dark with heavy lids, and I could tell dropping his guard for the moment was only bringing out exhaustion in him. Neither seemed like men who had just escaped a threat. They seemed, instead, disappointed and subdued.

My own resolve to leave, lessening. If I left, not coming back, ever, I'd never know what had happened, what the old man had done, what Acie's part was, who had married Acie way back when, what Acie was doing with a painting and a drawing by Max Beckmann. Leaving Acie now—his, well, frailty—no, a little longer, then I'll leave.

"Girl you should go," Acie said, looking through the stack of records beside him. The Byas had ended, and the needle was making its thwack sound in the eccentric.

And now, stubbornness. His sending me here and there for days. I was due an explanation.

"I'd rather not," I said, princessy, knowing it.

"*What?*" I felt the fast pierce, fear of his anger, of falling from his favor, and knowing no reason, no cause, but I didn't move. "You in there messing with the Bowtie—some get-rich—"

He was inches from me. The man Wyans suddenly coughed, when he spoke it was with a low, calm voice. "Came back when I heard she called, Ace. Thought you were into another situation."

Acie quieted, still keeping his eye on me, hesitated. The dog Ma right beside him.

"Was. Then Washington come in, who may have eradicated our Iguana infestation," Acie said to Wyans, his voice lowered now. "Made him a pox about the Cabrini pint-size, one you said died." His eye let go of me and I felt a string go lax.

"Did anyone leave some art with you, Acie? Painting, maybe?"

Acie gave him the same look he'd given me when I'd asked if he was married to the woman I'd called, eyed Wyans who returned the gaze head-on. The snowman painting, the fish drawing. I knew where they were. But turning, without speaking, Acie steered himself toward, through the beads, we heard rustling, a clank, then Acie back through the jangling curtains, coming toward us, Kraft-papered objects in his hands, his holding them as though the fish was alive and rotting in his arms. The dog sat and watched, too, the small nub of its tail flicking. At Wyans, Acie put them on the bins and unwrapped them.

"Doodles by the noodle. The Ma's without the paws." Acie, scorning. "William had a batch of these things and now Philly has been cluttering the crib with these two."

"Philomena told me we could try to buy off Brady with them," Wyans said, gently. He looked from one to the next, appraising, thoughtful. "I guess there's no need now."

Acie snorted. "You got to be kidding me." His incredulity fixed on Wyans, and then on me. "Come here, girl." Acie, almost barking it, but I came around the bins, down the gate aisle. Nearing and smelling him again, the smell a kind of relief. In the store light, I could see the bald glare of the snowman, its vacuum. I'd know, I'd know.

"Do you know about these easel uglifiers?"

I'd watched the front for him. I'd made the call. And now he was asking me to help him with art, his regard fixing on me, fierce. "All I know is—" I said, "they're by a painter, a German. A German painter named Beckmann."

Another snort. "That's news."

"Max Beckmann. He died thirty years ago."

Wyans looked at the floor. Acie turned his girth to face me fully, his face tense and focused. "You—" Moving back to his stool, leaning against it, his orange torso bulging.

"So what hustle have you and my Tied in a Bow been running?"

"What?" *Now* I'd leave.

"You hear me. I need to know what you have been pulling with the fine art you do not know the first of."

The folds of his face were suddenly steel.

"*I* have no idea, Acie—what are *you* doing with *these?*"

For a moment, still fierce, then his mouth shutting and he was leaning to feed the dog a kibble. I, reminding myself to think. The dog kept her eyes fixed on him like a baby, chomping down on it, waiting, patiently, for another. Mange had made her haunches shiny. Under its armpits, the orange expanse of Acie's shirt was splotched, and I noticed for the first time a mole in the gap at his waist.

"Thought you needed to pee," Acie said without looking up. "Hurry up so as I can go."

Did he mean Wyans? Wyans was looking at me. "I don't need to pee, Acie," I said.

"Then I will be back." He straightened and headed for the back room.

Sentiment intensifies individuality into type, wrote Beckmann. And this is why, I thought, the picturesque didn't make it.

Wyans looked at me unguardedly, sadly, and back at his friend's retreating form.

It was one man playing tenor alone for two hours, in a sculpture garden, at dusk, in the summer, new idea to theme song to twelve-tone to trivial, easy breathing, easy legato, bossa nova, then on to the screech-honks, intensity like a thick cake, a flourless cake that would come into fashion about this time, after the two millionth mark was passed on the penning of "Is Jazz Dead?", in the heat of a Manhattan summer, far from Chicago, the Chicago mayor, a Harold Washington, dead and strung by his panties on the canvas of a young artist keen to make his mark. To cause a sensation—but the man was playing, back there, seven years from that moment at Acie's, in a crowd that pressed in and heard him over the garden walls, giving him room and not breathing, the spiral of a siren and the honking vehicles just weft, nothing but weft, he in and out like a golden thread one moment, a red braid the next, ideas so quick in succession they weren't ideas at all, just the pressure of distilled intelligence, breathed into a saxophone, his calling up the bridge at night alone, past midnight, newly mohawked, scales, it didn't matter, learning how to move, how to transform dirge to jingle and back again, what speed does, what $^4/_5$ feels like outside, alone, halfway to

Brooklyn in the dark when you're young, much younger than now, so much dashed already and alone but for the press of all you'd stumbled into with your sorry donkey tail and blindfold, your pernicious aspirations, your settling in only when moving the sound around, it skirting now and then into a lousy pocket, onto a dead plateau, just scooping it out again, moving it forward, breathing into it, long after quiche disappeared from the menus and yet before the el became the L, a particular kind of freedom irregardless.

{

"One for you." Wyans had thought I wanted a malt ale, and I did. "Mr. Bartender" on the turntable, Jimmy Witherspoon: *one scotch, one bourbon, one beer.* We clicked the can tabs.

"Not out yet?" Wyans nodded to the curtain. Acie had been in there since Wyans crossed to the store and back again.

"Mr. Bartender" came to its end and I put on Idris Muhammad, his *Kabsha,* the run-up into the first cut scissoring smooth, his drumming delicate here where later it would be sly, deep, urgent. Turned to the door from Acie's stool.

The window, the world, the pummeling white, the man coming in from the stairwell brushing the snow from him, the door open on Harnett.

"We started *the Contemporary because of him, for Chrissakes, Henry.*" *The man in the office Perkins and Will built is almost shouting into the telephone, sweeping as he does the Chicago skyline through the window before him without seeing it.* "*I was* present *when he as much as* admitted *that the Institute, and I quote, 'does not have room for fast Jews.' How are we supposed to humor him, Henry? I don't care if the museum's never out of debt, we're not taking a fucking penny.*"

On the other end of the telephone connection, the listener looks up at the Phyllis Bramson doodle taped beside the careening stack of books he intends to read. They're an avalanche waiting to happen, he thinks, as his hand takes the notes.

Acie

"Your son." So long ago it was, I cannot see her face in memory. Only his, like a cartoon, like a negroid Casper, wound up tight to ball and then he did not, sick and us on the edge of losing him. The hospital room being a locker with lights.

I hear him in the store, conversing, and I hear her say, "What are these, Harnett?" and I think of him in league with the Philly, of him knowing about the business my brother undertook with a wife. Bowtie and the college and fine arts and more whatnot. I think of him and the house. I need to pay my water bill but the dick does not comply.

My goings-away. I think of the involvement of Brady Bonner, what they have all unlikely cooked up together. Girl and he going on like crows in the front. A fine urination will solve the half of it, I think in my stoppage.

It is Wyans I should saddle with the inventory not the son who I should have gift-wrapped for the Iguana when I had been given the chance. The holes in the story do not count up by now.

Urine. Elixir. "The cup that clears today of past regrets and future

fears" as the Omar Khayyam said himself. I call the boy back to see his
maker in the crib but the crows do not even hear.

"—nothing to do with it!"

"But then how do you—"

"Bow tie!" I am out from the crib and seeing them an inch from the
other. So the girl found the liar in the boy, she got *some* sense. Wyans
standing by, cool and in his own, this is why I trust him to the inside.

Bowtie turns around his usual hangdog. "Bow tie." I let him change
his attention. "If you have been waiting for the inheritance you are
wasting your time," I say. "You are as disowned as a son could be, so
disowned you are not getting a *cutout* when I go. You can catch up
with Fearless Freddy and beg on him for cash. That is *one*.

"This is *two*. Seeing as you are not the legacy I had in mind I could
cut the bloodline without remorse. If you have chosen a life the other
branches of the Stevensons and various military personnels endorse
then they can provide you with your fallbacks.

"*Three.* You involve a hair of the Sally professionally or intimately
and you are dead." Wyans rousts himself now to regard me.

"*Four.* You have—"

"Ace, it's over Ace." Wyans has his low voice. "Hear what the boy
has to say."

So the bequeathment go toward my own coffin instead.

"We still haven't got all the pieces, Ace."

"This your business, Wyans?" Burning me. Babs Gonzalez used to tell he came upon a woman on the street beating her gentleman companion who held his eyes yelling from the red pepper she had thrown at him and that was why Babs ever after carried what he called the "pill box of pain." This had not gotten me more than a laugh at the time but I think lately I full missed that boat. A little of the pepper for the Bow now would suit.

Stung scalp, trade my dog for a satisfying piss, wheezed and half blind I know my own boil. Wyans looks at me like the firm man he is in spite of my hot head. With friends like—

The girl is straight up at the offspring, may be first time I have seen her steamed.

Were Bow Tie Mutt-you-fuck-you *not* my blood.

"Acie," the offspring starts, "Cindy. Let me tell you." Like sincere was his ticket. "Please."

Phone rings but I ignore it. "You got you an art diploma?" I ask the Bowtie who looks at me now without a waver. "I am waiting on you."

"Okay," says the Mutt-you. "Yes, I helped Philly and William when their dealer died."

Bagman indeed. "Knew the pharmaceuticals in this."

"No, *art* dealer, Acie. Grandma's paintings—and then Ivie's. Bud Depries did it—" now that is a name I have not heard for a while. "He's the one who sold the paintings for them. When he died they asked me for help, and I thought I could do it, thought I could give them a hand—"

The thought of Bud Depries and the Iguana being party to the intimacies of my brother is the stinger. "Mr. Hog-tied Bowtie, if you have been at league with the brick-man, I will—"

The offspring tries to convince himself, a hero. "They needed somebody, Acie. How was I to know?"

"Boy." He looks now blarey eyed like that old Casper self and I cannot help it, I get soft on him. "The one shaking my tree was the Iguana. Whose relation to this circus I want to know now."

"So that's why Acie got mugged?" The girl's voice quiet as a booster.

"I didn't know," Bowtie says. "How was I to know he'd go after him?" Wyans looks to the floor and Bow T sighs a big one at the girl. "Acie didn't have anything to do with it."

"I'm going on up the street, Ace, be back." Wyans pulls from the wall and out from the scene. "If you need anything, you can call me."

The crows at each other quiet their selves down like two confused hens. Dog Ma yips and the phone toots as Wyans shuts to the door. Receiver under the pile.

"Palace for the platters that matter," I say and hear a chuckle from the other end.

"Acie Stevenson, good day to you and I hope it got better." It is Harold Washington, man I am now indebted to and who I will pay with my vote and my considerable mouth. "Just checking to see that all is okay, Acie." I tell him no, thanks to him and he chuckles to himself again which could irritate me if I let it.

Crows turned hens are in their own worlds. School takes you so far, up and coming takes you so far, gets you to *imitation* but not to *origination*. Not to the advance troop. If you *originate*—

"There is more to my life you are welcome to improve," I say. "Anytime you are ready."

Harold Washington does his original chuckle again. "Vote and I'm on it. I'll be seeing you, Acie. Thanks for the Hinton."

"Harold." I hang up the phone.

My son could use a sump pump by the bins for the remorse. "I'm sorry, Acie."

"Bebop Shop pays you. You settle for that."

If you *originate* there may be nothing to show for it. When Bowtie closes his eyes he parades the goods he craves; I can see this from my stool clear as a movie. A picture of a life he carries in his head. The girl watches him, too, like she can see every expensive float. She is on the top of one, waving.

When the acting work started paying, Redd liked to open up the South Side place on a Sunday. We all trooped through *look at this and that* to the yard out back where he had the slow cook on and served it with silver. A thing or two he would show off, fruit of the labors, and then he got neighbor kids to do their pageant. Not Jerry Lewis the Cinderfella, not TV, not that he learned them, they cooked up the pageants themselves, nobody there but us who he always ran with back to DuSable itself. Women growing out not up, Chicken Tahiti and blackplate, some blasting some clean, always Johnny or Elvin or even Redd playing music on the sly, on the foldout chairs, Jerome with his card tricks getting an audience to pick up nickels and lay down dollar bills. This was where I met her, Bowtie's ma.

She had herself skin like silk. Voice a honker but skin like silk itself. Others paid good money to hear her warble, I would have paid her to sew shut that mouth, but it was a mouth to be withstood. She dewed up fast and we had a time of it, always, until she left. Until the arrival of Casper, and she with a fear of the ghosts. It was six years before she was convinced to visits.

A kestrel swoops onto the shore and wobbles toward a plastic bag washed up against an empty Tab can. Out on the promontory, paused in his car, the divorcing man looks from the kestrel to the school bus in the cul-de-sac, emptying its charges into two scraggly strands lined up at the planetarium's door. The head of a small boy still remains in the window toward the back of the bus, and the man watches as an adult, headless in his view, walks the aisle back toward the boy. It is impossible for the man to tell if the adult is a woman or a man until the woman bends over, and then he sees the glint of large hoop earrings in the long slant of light that also hits the boy's face, rendering the boy, for a moment, gold, too.

Cindy

Acie's sister-in-law left the painting and drawing with him when she returned to New York, and he hung them above the bins. They drew an occasional customer comment but he pretended not to care. I made his weekly deposits, and twice a month he'd ask me to put them in my own account and write a check to Philomena Stevenson because, he said, his brother left her no pension.

Although I knew from the size of his deposits it was foolhardy for him to keep so little take, I wrote the check and sent it on to her in New York and, as he asked, kept some of the money for my own pay. I needed it, but I knew this only fueled Acie's creditors. I knew because I answered when they called.

I liked working for him. While he napped I would play what I wanted to hear, and the rest of the time he'd play what I otherwise wouldn't have—Gene Ammons, Kenny Burrell, Sarah Vaughn. Away from it for a few days at exam time, I secretly missed the big bands and the bebop, the swooping show-off arrangements, and the sly ensembles.

Acie watched me like a hawk. Ma, the dog, died.

For some time after the showdown, Harnett only wanted to talk about his uncle and the paintings, turning the story over and over like a ball of thread looking for the loose end in between his scamming one thing or another. It wore on me, and we grew apart. Besides, I went out to hear music less. When I was away from Acie's, I studied or slept.

At the department, I worked on Beckmann and the lost drawings, then Ryder, then Barnett Newman. When there were clues in the paintings I used them, and when there weren't I took it as a challenge to invent my own. My presentations were well received, and at semester's end Professor Bartel told me the doctoral vote was pending my exams. How well I did surprised me most of all, and admittance to the doctoral program brought with it a stipend and a housing chit. I began to feel that I belonged.

My job at Acie's gave me cachet among certain of my colleagues who saw it as exotic. I can't judge them for this; after a long day of reading abstracts or compiling lists out of the International Bibliography of Periodical Literature, my growing repertoire of Acie anecdotes must have been a welcome diversion. *Ma's mange and Acie's scalp* . . . "*She'd sign a contract with anyone who come along with a pencil,*" he said . . . *a kid named Lester who started hanging around the store.* The stories were colorful and distorted; looking back, I know them now as a betrayal.

~

In August the idea of snow was laughable. The hot air rolled off the pavement in waves of overcharged particles; crossing the river nothing stirred but the water, plastered to its course by the weight of the heat. A mongrel, part-Lab, picked up my path just over the bridge and followed, weaving or swooning, its tongue out, its panting loud. We crossed the State Street lot together. Even the basement would be hot today.

The gate was drawn. I remember thinking *oversleep on a Monday he'll miss the reps,* I remember the precise, still darkness through the window, my foreboding. I used my key and opened up and found him.

Even though the dog had died in May, it was she the stillness seemed to lack, not he. Acie lay where he had fallen, one arm bent beside his head like a police outline; I knew from films that I should close his eyes but I was afraid to touch him. Traffic whirred beyond the door, the refrigerator kicked on. I should call Harnett, I thought, but when I got to the phone it was out—one of Record Palace's periodic shutoffs. I had tried to placate the phone company just last week.

Turning off the lights again, not facing him, I sat on Acie's stool and cried. After a long while I looked up at the drawing of the fish, thumbtacked to the wall, frame long gone, above the Coltrane stacks. In the half-light of the window the fish was not a fish but a shape, a shadowed strip cutting the composition in half. I found a Milt Hinton and Joe Williams with Capp Pierce and put them in a bag.

I wish I could say now that I called Harnett when I left the store; I had intended to. I called 911 and gave the operator the address and the information, but I would not give my name. With the drawing rolled in my hand and the bag with the LPs in my other, the gate locked behind me, I wanted to walk, which I did, woozily, until the paper felt damp in my palm and, passing a movie theater, it occurred to me that it was essential that I see a movie, *now*. On the marquee: *American Gigolo, Gloria, Stir Crazy, The Fog*. I chose *Gloria*, which opened in a cemetery, and I cried again, shielding the drawing with my purse. I stayed on, for *Stir Crazy*, conflating the Wilder playwright with Willy Wonka and laughing at the magic word, *shit*, with the show's other patron, six rows back. By the time I left, it was late afternoon. The sun was lower but the baking had been intense, and stepping out into it I was immediately wet. Next door was a bar and I drank.

When a teenager runs away from home, it does not mean she wants the home to run away from her. My training as a daughter had been spotty, even though now I was old enough to have known and done better.

I watched the newspaper, half hoping for an obituary. After four days Harnett called to make sure I knew; he was already cooking up the inventory's sale to the Bebop Shop but his voice cracked and halted. I said yes, I'd heard. Was he okay?

Eight months after Acie died, I woke on my professor's bathroom floor, an acid taste filling my mouth, the imprint of the small lime tiles on my cheek, trying to discern the tufted pink mat beneath my knees. Two years after Acie died—on the morning Harold Washington was inaugurated mayor of Chicago after an election in which the spirit of the city, on the sidewalks, in the stores, shifted overnight, wholly, perceptibly—I woke to find a strange man asleep, or rather *passed out*, beside me, and the fresh indent of another, a woman, who had risen to find a strange coffeemaker in a strange kitchen, mine.

Four years after his death, when I was on the verge of bankruptcy, Professor Bartel, by now the expert on Beckmann forgeries, could not declare my drawing a fake. Nonetheless, with its murky provenance, I couldn't sell it, and a year later, on the heels of eviction and this bankruptcy, I finally dried out. Six years after Acie died, my orals were rough in my new, sober, tongue-tied state, but the committee stamped me a doctor. A month later Mom magnanimously, finally, died.

Those who inherited the business of Walt Disney after the entrepreneur died built at long last a large warehouse on the site of the old SRO hotel and the basement record store, razed years ago. On State Street between Chicago's Gold Coast and its Hubbard Street galleries, the Disney Company opened, in a February, mid-nineties, an indoor super-arcade, a theme park within walls, in which the soundtrack was the beeping and blipping of the many machines, the whooshing of the simulated waterfall, the bonks of the rubber mallets on the rubber blocks, the roars of the simulated monsters in the virtual reality booths. Reporting for work, the ticket-takers in the morning triggered the noise as they tripped the elevator's light cell. This was fifteen years after Acie died, and by this time I saw no one who had known him.

I saw no one who had known him, but I spoke of him all the time. These were my stories, my past, and they impressed others. That I borrowed them, that I used them, that I used even the memory of him, I am aware. It is the inside of it, what I have tried so unsuccessfully to tell you here—so distorted as it still is, so inadequate—it is what knowing Acie was that I alone know. This, in short, is the fact. I loved him, I made of him an idea, an idea with currency for myself, and he died. Now, still, I miss him.

Al Capone saved Duke Ellington from threats of violence, but chained Earl Hines to a $150 a week contract that was constructed to last forever. Capone, through his Grand Terrace manager, had a contract with Hines that literally would not permit Hines to use his own name if he attempted to leave the Grand Terrace plantation. His contract was perpetual: if Ed Fox died, Hines would become the personal property of Fox's widow . . .

DEMPSEY J. TRAVIS,
AN AUTOBIOGRAPHY OF BLACK JAZZ

Selected Playlist

Joni Mitchell. "Twisted." *Court and Spark*. Elektra/Asylum 1001–2.

Tim Buckley. "Gypsy Woman." *happy sad*. Elektra 7559 74045 2.

Art Ensemble of Chicago. *Nice Guys*. ECM 1126.

Lester Bowie. "The Great Pretender," "It's Howdy Doody Time," *The Great Pretender*. ECM 1209.

Teddy Edwards. *Teddy's Ready*. Contemporary 7583.

The Brecker Brothers. *Back to Back*. Arista 4061.

Sal Nistico. "Trouble," *Neo Nistico*. w/ Roy Haynes, Ronnie Mathews. Bee Hive BH 7006.

Richie Cole. "Stormy Weather," *New York Afternoon: Alto Madness*. Muse 5119.

Elvin Jones. *Remembrance*. MPS 15523.

Ornette Coleman. "Lonely Woman," *The Shape of Jazz to Come*. Rhino 1317.

Lester Bowie. "Lonely Woman," *Fast Last*. Muse MR–5055.

Cab Calloway. *The Hi-De-Ho Man*. RCA Starline 61079.

Abbey Lincoln. *People in Me*. Inner City 6040.

Sarah Vaughan. *Sarah Vaughan with Clifford Brown*. Emarcy.

Art Blakey. *Orgy in Rhythm, vol. 1*. Blue Note 1554.

Billy Harper. "Priestess," *Billy Harper Quintet in Europe*. Soul Note
1001.

Joe Williams. "Joe's Blues," *Live at the Century Plaza*. Concord 4072.

Art Blakey and the Jazz Messengers. "Lift Every Voice and Sing," *In
My Prime*. Timeless 118.

Art Blakey and the Jazz Messengers. *Live at Birdland, vols. 1–3*. Blue
Note 5037–9.

Art Blakey and the Jazz Messengers. *Recorded Live at Bubba's*. Who's
Who in Jazz 21019.

Jackie McLean Sextet. *Monuments*. RCA AFLI 3230.

Dizzy Gillespie. *Oop-pop-a-dah*. Victor 202480.

Muhal Richard Abrams. "D Song," *Live at Montreux 1978*. Arista
Novus 3007.

Frank Sinatra with Count Basie and His Orchestra. "Fly Me to the
Moon," *It Might as Well Be Swing*. Reprise FS–1012.

Mills Brothers. *The Mills Brothers Live*. Dot DP–25783.

Dexter Gordon. "I Should Care," *Lionel Hampton with Dexter
Gordon*. Who's Who in Jazz WWLP 21011.

Dexter Gordon. "I Told You So," "Body and Soul," *Manhattan
Symphonie*. Columbia JC 35608.

Dexter Gordon. "The Apartment," "Antabus," *The Apartment*.
Steeplechase SCS 1025.

Johnny Griffin. "I Should Care," "Autumn Leaves," "Monk's Dream," "When We Were One," *Return of the Griffin.* Galaxy 5117.

Johnny Griffin and Dexter Gordon Quintet. "Body and Soul," *Jazz Undulation.* Joker UPS 2058.

The O'Jays. "What am I Waiting For?", *Survival.* Philadelphia International 33150.

Sonny Rollins. *Horn Culture.* Milestone OJC 314.

Art Ensemble of Chicago. *Live from Mandel Hall.* Delmark DE 432.

John Coltrane. "India," *Impressions.* Impulse! MCAL–5887.

Ray Bryant Trio. "Stick with it," *All Blues.* Pablo 2310 820.

Art Pepper. *Art Pepper Today.* Galaxy OJC–474.

Paquito D'Rivera. *Blowin'!* Columbia 37374.

Arthur Blythe. *In the Tradition.* Columbia JC 36300.

McCoy Tyner, Ron Carter, and Sonny Rollins. *The Milestone Jazzstars.* Milestone M–55006.

Gato Barbieri and Dollar Brand. *Confluence.* Arista 1003.

Peaches & Herb. "Reunited," *2 Hot!* Polydor 2391378.

Milt Hinton. *The Trio.* Chiaroscuro 188.

Mary Lou Williams. *Mary Lou Williams Quartet featuring Don Byas.* Crescendo Records CNP 9030.

Jimmy Witherspoon. "One Scotch, One Bourbon, One Beer," *Mean Old Frisco.* Prestige 7855.

Idris Muhammad. *Kabsha.* Theresa 101.

Permissions

Acknowledgments

I owe a lot to many for this book, slight as it is. It would not have been written without the assistance of Janet Coleman, Maggie Paley, Harvey Shapiro, Brad Kessler, Hugh Seidman, Beth Bosworth, Philip Furmanski, and Claire Cummings. Thank you. Editors like Fiona McCrae and Anne Czarniecki, and agents like Bill Clegg, are not supposed to exist any longer; I still can't believe my fortune in working with them. I am also grateful to Bob Koester and Wayne Segal, who had considerable patience with my questions; to April Gornik and Eric Fischl for both a quiet space and sage readings; and to the John Simon Guggenheim Foundation for its generous support.

For their readings and their coachings I am ever grateful to Aldon Nielsen, Ngugi wa Thiong'o, Darcey Steinke, David Trinidad, Richard Frost, Binnie Kirshenbaum, Claudia Rankine, James Salter, Estelle Leontief, Steve Martin, Mary Jo Bang, Howard Mandel, Lawrence Joseph, Yusef Komunyakaa, Nina Frost, Ira Silverberg, Rick Moody, Tom Hooper, Roger Ferlo, Mark Strand, Simon Armitage, Jean Hanff Korelitz, Lan Samantha Chang, and to Dan and Julie Wheeler.

Stephen Jay Gould and Annette Weiner were generous with their readings, and I miss them very much. Thank you, too, to the Yaddo Corporation, Hector Rivera, Peter Shannon, Carol Morrow, Lynda Smith, Joe Juliano, Cesar Coronado, Jorge Lugo, Joseph Giordano, Giovanni di Salvo, Nevil Rodriguez and Seleh Mohamed for providing space and quiet.

Working on this book gave me an excuse to read a lot of extraordinary others. I particularly would like to acknowledge my debt to the Chicago-based books of Dempsey J. Travis. Real places and musicians' names have been used in my story, but all events depicted in the book, as well as the principal characters, their speeches, and their experiences are invented.

Finally, in love and honor, in memory of William Whitney and of William Chavers, who are now present only to God.

Susan Wheeler's books of poetry include *Bag 'o' Diamonds,*
Smokes, Source Codes, and *Ledger.* She lives in the New York
area.

The text of *Record Palace* has been set in Warnock Pro, a typeface designed by Robert Slimbach for Adobe Systems in 2000. Book designed by Wendy Holdman. Composition by Stanton Publication Services, Inc. Manufacturing by Friesens on acid-free paper.